Other *Leisure* books by Peter Dawson:

DARK RIDERS OF DOOM
ANGEL PEAK
FORGOTTEN DESTINY
GHOST BRAND OF THE WISHBONES
LONE RIDER FROM TEXAS
CLAIMING OF THE DEERFOOT
RATTLESNAKE MESA

GHOST OF THE CHINOOK

A Western Quintet

PETER DAWSON

LEISURE BOOKS NEW YORK CITY

A LEISURE BOOK®

August 2007

Published by special arrangement with Golden West Literary Agency.

Dorchester Publishing Co., Inc.
200 Madison Avenue
New York, NY 10016

ISBN-10: 0-8439-5900-2
ISBN-13: 978-0-8439-5900-0

Printed in the United States of America.

Visit us on the web at www.dorchesterpub.com.

TABLE OF CONTENTS

Spawn of Yuma

Jonathan Hurff Glidden was born in Kewanee, Illinois and was graduated from the University of Illinois with a degree in English literature. In his career as a Western writer he published sixteen novels and over 120 short novels and short stories for the magazine market. His Peter Dawson novels are noted for their adept plotting, interesting and well-developed characters, their authentically researched historical backgrounds, and stylistic flair. The first Peter Dawson novel, *The Crimson Horseshoe*, won the Dodd, Mead Prize as the best Western of the year 1941 and ran serially in Street & Smith's *Western Story Magazine* prior to book publication. *Dark Riders of Doom*, a story collection, and *Rattlesnake Mesa* are among his more recent book publications. "Spawn of Yuma" first appeared in *Western Story Magazine* (5/11/40).

I

The man who lay belly down and half covered with snow at the lip of the *rincón* looked dead but for the thin fog of vapor that betrayed his breathing. His curly, straw-colored hair was powdered with snow, and his outfit—light canvas windbreaker, brown vest over thin blue cotton shirt, Levi's, and boots worn through at the soles—made a mockery of the below-zero wind. The bronze of his lean, beard-stubbled face showed two colorless spots along his high cheek bones, a clear sign of frostbite. His lips were blue, and his long-fingered hands, one clenching a sizable rock, were clawed in a stiffness that suggested death. His brown eyes, squinted against the wind-riding particles of snow, were very much alive. They stared unwinkingly into the fading light of dusk, regarding a rider on a roan horse threading his way through a sparse growth of timber seventy yards below. A wariness was in the eyes, the wariness of the hunted animal. Once, when the rider reined in at the near margin of the trees and looked directly above, the hand that held the rock lifted an inch or two out of the snow.

That gesture and that weapon, feebly menacing when compared to the Winchester in the saddle scabbard of the horseman, remained fixed until the rider had disappeared into the snow haze. It gave a small hint of the dogged energy that had driven Bill Ash these last four days and three nights. The fact that he now laboriously thrust his body up to a crawling position and started dragging himself toward the dying coals of a fire at the bottom of the *rincón* was further evidence of it. He knew only that the fire's warmth meant life to him. And he wanted very much to live.

Stark singleness of purpose had brought Bill Ash in those four days and three nights the 227 miles from Yuma's mild winter to the bitter one in these Wild Horse Hills. He had walked off the penitentiary farm and escaped on a bay gelding stolen from the picket line of the fort, regardless of the knowledge that he was unarmed and that his outfit was too light to warm him against the weather into which he was heading. Last night, when the gelding had thrown him and bolted, the compelling drive that was bringing him back home hadn't weakened. He'd thrown up a windbreak of cedar boughs and built a small fire, gambling his luck against the fierce beginnings of a blizzard.

Somehow he had lived out the night. Today he had crossed the peaks afoot. This was the sixth fire he had built to drive out the pleasant numbness of slow death by freezing. As he crawled to the fire and held his stiffened hands to within three inches of the coals, Bill Ash knew that it had been worth it.

For three miles to the south and out of sight in the gathering night and the falling snow lay the town of Rimrock, his goal. The blizzard that had so nearly claimed his life would in turn work to save it now. The gelding would be found and identified. The snow would blot out his sign. No law officer, even if he were interested, would believe that a man unarmed and afoot had been able to outlive the storm.

It took Bill Ash a quarter of an hour to thaw his hands enough to move his fingers, another thirty minutes before he felt it was safe to take off his boots and snow-rub the circulation back into his frostbitten feet. The pain in his feet and legs was a torture that dispelled some of the drowsiness brought on by cold and hunger. An hour and ten minutes after crawling back from the edge of the *rincón*, he was walking over it and stumbling down the slope toward the trees where the rider had passed. The roan's sign wasn't yet quite blotted out, the hoof marks still showing as faint depressions in the white snow blanket. Bill examined the tracks out of curiosity, remembering something vaguely familiar about the roan but still puzzled as to who the rider might have been. Well back in the trees where the wind didn't have its full sweep, he found the sign clearer. At first sight of it he placed the horse. The indentation of the right rear hoof was split above the shoe mark. The roan had once belonged to his father. He wondered idly, before he went on, who owned the horse now and what errand had brought the owner up here into the hills at dusk to ride into the teeth of the blizzard when any man in his right mind would have been at home hugging a fire.

*   *   *

Two minutes after dark, ten minutes short of seven o'clock, Bill Ash stood in an alley that flanked Rimrock's single street and peered in through the lighted and dusty back window of a small, frame building. The window looked into an office. Two men were in the room. Bill Ash knew both of them. Ed Hoyt, whose law office this was, sat with his back to the window in a swivel chair behind his roll-top desk, arms upraised and hands locked comfortably behind his head. He was smoking an expensive-looking Havana cigar. The cigar and the glowing fire door of the stove across the room were the two things that made it hardest for Bill to wait patiently, his tall frame trembling against the driving snow and the cold. The other man, old Blaze Leslie, was wizened and stooped but every inch the man to wear the sheriff's star that hung from a vest pocket beneath his coat.

Neither man had changed much in the last three years. Ed Hoyt was, if anything, more handsome than ever. His dark hair was grayer at the temples, Bill noticed, a quirk of pigmentation for Hoyt had barely turned thirty. The lawyer's broadcloth suit and the fancy-stitched boot he cocked across one knee were visible signs of affluence. Ed Hoyt had obviously done well at practicing law. But aside from this new-found prosperity, he was the same man who had defended Bill three years ago and tried to save him a term at Yuma. Blaze Leslie was as unchanged as a slab of hard rim rock, his grizzled old face wearing a familiar harassed and dogmatic look. Bill couldn't hate him, even though it was Blaze who had arrested him on the false charge that had sent him to prison.

About twenty minutes after Bill stepped to the

window, the sheriff tilted his wide-brimmed hat down over his eyes, turned up the collar of his sheep-lined coat, and went out the door into the street. Bill waited until Blaze's choppy boot tread had faded down the plank walk out front before knocking at the office's alley door. He heard the scrape of Ed Hoyt's chair inside and stood a little straighter. Then the door opened, and he was squinting into the glare of an unshaded lamp in Ed Hoyt's hand. He felt a rush of warm air hit him in the face, its promise so welcome that the sigh escaping his wide chest was a near sob.

He said, even-toned—"It's me, Ed . . . Bill Ash."— and heard the lawyer catch his breath.

Hoyt drew back out of the doorway. "I'll be damned," he muttered in astonishment.

Bill stepped in, pushing the door shut behind him. He did not quite understand the set unfriendliness that had replaced the astonishment in Ed Hoyt's face. Ed was clearly surprised and awed, but there was no word or sign of welcome from him.

Bill said uncertainly, trying to put an edge of humor in his voice: "Don't get to believin' in ghosts, Ed. It's really me."

Hoyt moved quickly across the room, reaching back to set the lamp on his desk and wheeling in behind it to open the top drawer. His hand rose swiftly into sight again and settled into line with Bill. It was fisting a double-barreled Derringer.

"Stay where you are, Ash," he said tonelessly.

It took Bill several seconds to realize that this was really the man he had once considered his best friend, the man who had defended him at his trial. His hands were thrust deeply into the pockets of his canvas jacket, and he clenched them hard, the only betrayal of the bitter disappointment that gripped him.

"I'm cold," he said mildly. "Mind if I soak up some of your heat?" He stepped obliquely across the room, putting his back to the stove's friendly warmth. Only then could he trust himself to add: "I didn't expect this sort of a howdy, Ed."

Ed Hoyt's round and handsome face hardened. "Blaze just left," he said. "He's got the word from Yuma. He never thought you could make it through the storm."

"I had to," Bill told him, then nodding toward the Derringer that still centered on his chest: "Do you need that?"

"There's a reward out for you. I'm a law-abiding citizen." The statement came flatly, without a trace of friendliness.

Bill's brows raised in a silent query. He was able to stand quietly now, to keep his knees and shoulders from shaking against the chill that had a moment ago cut him to the marrow. The stove's heat was warming his back through the thin canvas.

"And you were so sure I was innocent!" he drawled.

"It's been three years," Hoyt reminded him. "I haven't found a shred of proof that you didn't kill that man, that you didn't steal your father's herd."

"You made it convincing enough at the trial. They didn't hang me."

"If I had it to do over again, I'd do it differently! You were guilty, Bill. Guilty as hell!"

Bill's mind was beginning to work with its normal agility. The first thing, of course, was to put

Hoyt in his place. All at once he knew how he was going to do it. He said: "Ed, I've got my hand wrapped around a Forty-Five." He nodded down to his right hand thrust deeply in a pocket. "Want to shoot it out or will you toss that iron across here?"

The change that came over Ed Hoyt's face was striking. His ruddy skin lost color, the eyes widened a trifle and dropped to regard the bulge of Bill's pocket. Then, after a moment's indecision, his nerve left him and the Derringer moved out of line. He dropped it. Bill, stepping across to kick the weapon out of the lawyer's reach, said dryly: "These ladies' guns are tricky. You're lucky it didn't go off." He stooped to pick the weapon from the floor, reaching with his right hand and smiling thinly at the ready anger that crossed Hoyt's face on seeing his hand emerge from the pocket empty. As he straightened again, he nodded toward the chair behind the desk. "Sit!" he ordered curtly. "I've got to know some things before I leave here."

Hoyt lowered himself into the chair, sitting stiffly under the threat of Bill's right hand that was once more in his pocket but now armed. A change rode over him. His anger disappeared, and he said ingratiatingly: "I didn't mean it, Bill. Your steppin' in here like that set me on . . . "

"Forget it!" Bill cut in, irritated at the show of hypocrisy. "Tell me how it happened, how he died?"

"Your father?" Hoyt asked.

Bill nodded. "I read about it in a Tucson paper. That's why I'm here, why I busted out to get here."

"They found him below the rim near your place," Hoyt said, adding: "Or rather, that's where he died. The rim was caved in where he went over. They dug until they found the horse and saddle. The saddle was bloody. That was enough proof."

Bill's lean face had shaped itself into hard, predatory lines. His voice held a thin edge of sarcasm when he next spoke. "Looks like the Ash family travels with hard luck. The paper said the old man and Tom Miles had had an argument and that Miles was missing. Any more evidence that he did it?"

Hoyt showed a faint surprise. "I thought you knew. They arrested Miles three days ago. He claims he didn't do it."

Inside Bill there was an instant's constriction of muscle that gradually relaxed to leave him weak and feeling his exhaustion and hunger. The thought that had driven him on through these four bleak and empty days had been the urge to hunt down Tom Miles, his father's killer, the man he suspected of having framed him with murder and rustling three years ago. To find now that the law had cheated him of a meeting with Miles, of the satisfaction of emptying a gun at the man, was a bitter, jolting disappointment. He leaned against the edge of the desk, his knees all at once refusing to support his weight.

Ed Hoyt went on: "Miles was tried yesterday. They hang him day after tomorrow."

Bill's face shaped a twisted smile. "Saves me the job." There was something more he wanted to know about his father's old enemy. "What evidence did they have against him?"

"All they needed. He and your father were seen riding toward the hills together that afternoon. They'd had an argument a couple days before. Something about whose job it was to fix a broken fence. I don't believe Miles was guilty. I defended him." He raised his hands, palms outward in a gesture of helplessness. "I couldn't convince the jury. Your father was a big man in this country. People wanted to see his murder paid off."

There was a long interval of silence, one in which Bill felt the keen disappointment of not having been able to deal out his own justice. Abruptly he thought of another thing. "What about Linda?"

The mention of that name brought a frown to Ed Hoyt's face, one that reminded Bill of the nearly forgotten rivalry that had existed three years ago between himself and the lawyer. It had been a strange thing that Bill should love the daughter of his enemy, now his father's killer, and stranger still that his best friend, Ed Hoyt, should be Tom Miles's choice of a son-in-law and that their rivalry at courtship had seemingly never interfered with their high regard for each other.

"Linda's taking it pretty well," the lawyer answered. "We're . . . we're to be married as soon as this is over."

A stab of regret struck through Bill, yet he could speak sincerely: "You'll make her happy, Ed. It's a cinch I couldn't . . . now."

Linda must have known then that waiting for his parole from Yuma was as futile as trying to get her father's permission to marry an ex-convict. He had written her a year ago telling her as much. His letter had been casual, intended to convince her that he no longer loved her, that she wasn't still his one reason for wanting to live. Gradually, through this past year, he had put her from his mind. It had changed him, hardened him, this realization that the one thing in life that really mattered was being denied him. But it had seemed the only fair thing to do, to remove himself from her life when to remain a part of it would have been too great a handicap for her to endure. "What about Miles's ranch?" he now asked in a new and gruffer voice.

"I'll run it, along with my business." Hoyt leaned forward in his chair. "That brings up another thing, Bill. Have you heard about your father's new will?"

Bill shook his head. The lawyer reached over and thumbed through a stack of papers on his desk, selecting one, a legal form, and handing it across. "That's a copy. Your father had it made up two days before he died. The original's temporarily lost. Blaze Leslie's going to try and find it at your layout once this business is over. It must be somewhere in your father's papers."

Bill read through the two pages, not believing what he saw the first time and going over it again. Here, in black and white, was an indictment that aged him ten years. First came old Bob Ash's blunt statement that he was disowning his son. He gave his reason. In the three years since Bill had been in prison, he'd been convinced that his son had betrayed him by stealing his cattle and killing one of his crew. In his father's own salty language were written the details of disposing of Brush Ranch in case of his death. A value of five thousand dollars, less than a tenth of its worth, was set on the outfit. The buyer was named as Ed Hoyt. The reason, bluntly given, was that Ed Hoyt had performed loyal legal services in trying to save Bob Ash's son from a deserved death. For that loyalty Ed Hoyt was to be given title to the ranch on a mere token payment. The $5,000 was to be divided equally between three members of the crew who had seen long service on the Brush spread.

The names of these three men wavered before Bill's glance. He realized abruptly that tears of anger and hurt were in his eyes. He crumpled the paper and looked away until he got control of himself.

Ed Hoyt must have detected this emotion in him for he said: "I'm sorry to break it to you this way. Now you know why I think the way I do, that you were guilty, after all. Your father convinced me."

"But his letters would have said something about it!" Bill argued. Then he saw how futile that protest was. He tossed the wadded sheets onto the desk, giving way to the bitterness that was in him. "I'm headed out, Ed." He nodded to indicate the alley door. "I'll keep an eye on you through this window for a few minutes to make sure you don't head up the street to send Blaze out after me."

Hoyt's face blanched. "I wouldn't turn you in now, Bill. You deserve another chance. I won't give you away."

"No?" Bill said dryly, and let it go at that. The one word was eloquent of his distrust and bitterness. As he stepped to the door leading out to the alley, he paused a moment. "Tell Linda I'm wishing her luck." Then, catching the lawyer's sober nod, he was gone out the door.

He stood for several seconds outside the window, watching that Ed Hoyt didn't move out of his chair. He turned up the collar of his light jacket and put his back to the drive of the wind, feeling the cold settle through him once more in a wave that completed his utter misery. No longer did he have the will to move, to fight, even to live. He knew he should get away from here, put miles between him and Rim-rock tonight, for Ed Hoyt couldn't be trusted not to go to the sheriff once he thought the fugitive gone. Yet it didn't seem to matter now what happened. The law had cheated him twice, this time of the one thing that mattered, his chance to exact vengeance on Tom Miles, his father's murderer. In two more days the law would call Tom Miles to answer for his crime at the end of a rope.

Strangely enough, it gave Bill little satisfaction to think that the man was to die this way. Miles and old Bob Ash had been bitter enemies since they had come to this country. First there had been a long feud over the boundary that divided their outfits. Then, after years of fairly peaceful neighborliness, had come the matter of Bill's and Linda's feeling for each other. Bill's father hadn't minded, but Tom Miles had, forbidding his daughter to see the son of his old enemy. Suddenly, in swift and unalterable succession, had come Bill's arrest on the charge of stealing his own father's cattle and murdering a Brush crewman, the trial and Ed Hoyt's inspired de-fense that had saved Bill from the hangman's noose and instead sent him to the penitentiary for life. Then the three long years at Yuma. Bill had always suspected Tom Miles of the frame-up as the surest means of keeping his daughter from marrying an Ash. Now that the law had finally caught up with Miles, he was sure of it.

II

Bill Ash could never afterward quite explain the half-insane impulse that prompted him to turn abruptly away from Ed Hoyt's window and stride along the alley in the direction of the jail. He knew only that a moment before his right hand, reaching into his pocket, had touched the cold steel of the Derringer. He had a weapon, a weapon that could kill a man at short range. He knew that a small window was set in the rear of the jail's single cell and that Tom Miles deserved to die without a chance.

He came abreast the low, stone jail. A rain barrel sat under a downspout within three feet of the high-barred window. Faint light showed through the window, which meant that Blaze Leslie was still in his office that occupied the front half of the building's one long room. That didn't matter, nothing mattered but this chance of seeing Tom Miles, defenseless, die by a hand he had betrayed.

Bill climbed onto the barrel, feeling its weight of solid ice hold steady beneath him. He leaned over

and looked in the glass of the window as he was
reaching for the Derringer. The bars of the cell's
front wall drew a lined pattern halfway up along the
narrow room. Beyond the bars sat Blaze Leslie,
boots cocked up on his battered desk. He was reading a paper with a lamp at his elbow. On this side of
the bars was outlined a cot and a figure lying on it.
Tom Miles was stretched out on his back, knees up,
arms folded across his chest. Bill's face took on a sar-
donic grin as he raised the Derringer and swung it
down, about to break out the glass and take his careful aim at Tom Miles. At the precise instant he
caught a whisper of sound behind him. He pushed
back from the window and turned his head in time
to see a shadow darker than the snow-whipped
night moving toward him. Then, suddenly, a weight
drove in at his legs and pushed him off balance.

He was falling. He reached out with both hands
to break his fall, dropping the Derringer. He lit
hard, one shoulder taking his weight. A figure
moved in over him as he tried to roll out of the way.
A glancing blow struck him on the head and
stunned him for a moment. Then the cold muzzle of
a gun was thrust into his face and a low voice said:
"Quiet. Or I'll kill you."

Bill recognized the voice instantly. He forgot the
gun and the slacking off of tension brought a reac-
tion in him that started every muscle in his body
trembling. He was coldly sane once more and
ashamed of the impulse that had guided him here.

He was about to speak when the voice said again:
"Get onto your feet." He obeyed. Then: "Your hands!
Keep them up!" He raised his hands to the level of
his shoulders.

The figure, a full head shorter than his own, moved around behind him. The thrust of a gun nudged him in the spine in a silent command that started him walking along the alley. When he had taken three strides, the pressure of the gun moved him over toward a slant-roofed woodshed behind the store that adjoined the jail. The voice said: "Open the door and go in."

He reached out, loosened the hasp on the door, and stepped inside. It was warm in here. The air was heavy with the reek of burned coal oil. The hard pressure of the gun left his spine, and he heard movement behind him. The door hinges squeaked, and the cold draft of the wind abruptly died out. The flare of a match behind threw his shadow across a stack of split cedar in the shed's far corner. Then the match's flare steadied and the voice said: "Turn around. Keep your hands up."

As Bill turned, he had to squint against the glare of a lantern held at a level with his face. Beyond the lantern he saw a face, and a yearning suddenly leaping up to him made him breathe: "Linda."

He caught the quick changes on her oval, finely chiseled face. Disbelief and wonderment widened her eyes. There was a flash of recognition and then that, too, disappeared. "How do you know my name?" Linda Miles demanded flatly.

He was held speechless a moment, groping for understanding. Finally it came, and he laughed uneasily, realizing how Yuma and these past four days must have changed him. His face was gaunt and bearded, and his hair, long uncut, gave her no clue to his identity. Three years at hard labor and a diet only sufficient to keep him alive had thinned him down to a wiry toughness that made him a shadow of what he had once been. Before he could answer, she said again sharply: "How do you know me?"

"Look again, Linda."

Once again his voice prompted that flash of recognition in her. He could see it come to her eyes, die out, and then flare alive again, this time more strongly. She said in a voice barely audible: "But it can't be."

"It is, Linda."

The lantern lowered slowly until it rested on the floor. Now he could see her better. The heavy gun she was holding lowered to her side. Her hazel eyes were wide, tear-filled, as she finally understood what his being out there at the jail window had meant. Suddenly, choking back a sob, she cried: "Bill! Bill, he didn't do it!" He made no answer. She came close to him, her two hands taking a strong grip on his arms. She shook him fiercely. "I know, Bill! You must have faith in me."

Her nearness, the fragrance of her hair, made him want to take her in his arms. He didn't. He was remembering Ed Hoyt, knowing that what had been between himself and this girl could never come back. But still he couldn't trust himself to speak.

Her look gradually changed to one of alarm. "Bill! You're half frozen! You're thin! You're sick!"

He shook his head and smiled down at her. "Not sick any more. Just a little hungry. Tired, too, maybe."

Her hand raised and ran gently over his beard-stubbled face. "I didn't think I could ever be this happy again," she murmured. Then, before he could grasp the depth of emotion that lay behind her

words, her hand ran down over his thin jacket, and
she said: "You've been out in this storm . . . in this?"

"I'm all right now," he told her.

"You're not!" Abruptly she reached down and
moved the lantern to one side, indicating a pile of
gunny sacking on the floor closest to the wall that
faced the back of the jail. A board had been pulled
loose near the floor.

"I've spent the last two nights here," she explained. "Watching, hoping I'd catch someone
sneaking into the jail. I thought you were the man I
was after, the man who had framed Dad." When she
caught the look of disbelief he couldn't hide, she
said: "Never mind. I don't expect you to take it all
in. But lie down there and rest, and we can talk later
when I get back. The lantern will warm you."

"Where are you going?" he asked as she turned to
the door.

"To get you the best meal in town," Linda answered as she went out.

He sat weakly down on the improvised bed. He
moved the lantern closer, relishing its warmth. As he
lay back on the gunny sacking, he realized how im-
plicitly she must trust him to leave him like this,
within striking distance of her father. He closed his
eyes. The knowledge of having lived out his dream
of seeing this girl once again was a tonic that
calmed the riot and confusion in him. He no longer
felt alone. He was asleep in less than ten seconds.

An instinctive awareness made him open his eyes at
the sound of the door hinges grating against the
moaning of the wind that whipped the corners of

the shed. Linda came into the light. She knelt alongside him, laying a tray covered with a cloth on the
floor. "I'm thankful to have a friend or two left," she
said. "Charley won't talk." She was speaking of
Charley Travers, owner of the lunch room. She
added: "You didn't tell me you'd seen Ed. I met him
on his way to the jail to tell the sheriff you were in
town. I made him promise he wouldn't." She smiled
in a way that showed him a deep hurt that lay within
her. "He . . . he told you we were to be married?"

Bill nodded. "He's a good man, Linda."

She shrugged lifelessly. "Good enough, I've decided. Or rather, Dad has. I'm going through with it
for Dad."

Bill knew that much must be left unsaid between
them. To hide his own thoughts, he reached down
and took the cloth from the tray. "You never know
how good food is until you've gone without it,
Linda," he drawled.

She had brought him a bowl of bean soup, steak
and potatoes, and a generous pot of steaming coffee.
He tried to eat slowly, knowing that his stomach
would rebel at this full meal after having gone so
long on next to nothing—his last meal had been the
hindquarters of a tough old jack rabbit scorched
over the flames of a fire made of wet wood. He ate
the steak first, drank half the soup, and then had his
first cup of coffee. Pushing the tray back, he said:
"The rest can wait."

"I didn't forget this, either," she told him, and
took a sack of tobacco from a pocket of her wool
jacket.

He had built his first cigarette in four days and

was taking in his first satisfying lungful of smoke before she spoke again: "You came back to kill Dad, didn't you, Bill?"

He nodded, reminded once again of the gulf that had widened between them in these three years. "I had a gun," he said, deciding not to tell her how he came to have the Derringer and of Ed Hoyt's strange action.

His honest answer brought a look to her hazel eyes that implored him to understand and believe. She said softly: "I know, I know exactly how you feel. But I know Dad didn't kill your father, as surely as I know he didn't frame you three years ago. The reason I know is that I was with Dad that afternoon your father died. I had ridden over to the Hansens' to take their new baby some things. I met Dad and your father on the way back, there at the fork in the trails. Dad and I watched your father ride on. Then we came home. Dad wasn't out of my sight that whole afternoon and evening until Blaze Leslie came to arrest him that night."

As she spoke, Bill's long frame went rigid. He searched her face now, loathing himself for the brief moment he had thought he could read deception in its strong, clean lines. No, Linda Miles would never lie to him. Too much lay between them to make that possible. Suddenly a full understanding came to him. It left him weak and uncertain. For an instant he felt lost, as though blind and groping for a solid footing that had been swept from under him. Linda must have read what lay behind the dogged set of his face, for she went on: "I was going to write, to try and explain. This is better, your hearing me say it. I tried to tell them at the trial, but they wouldn't listen." Her head came up in a proud look of defiance. "Now I'm trying to make you believe."

Bill heard himself saying: "I do believe it, Linda. You'd never lie to me."

A wave of emotion swept over her. Gratitude and tenderness were in the look she gave him. "You *do* believe me?" she said humbly. Then she choked back a sob and buried her face in her hands. "Nothing else matters now, Bill."

Because this girl had been denied him, because he remembered Ed Hoyt in this moment, Bill didn't reach out to touch her as he longed to. Instead he said flatly: "Then who pushed my father over the rim?"

Her face tilted up to him again. She visibly restrained the tenderness that had been in her a moment ago, seeming to realize the force of will that was guiding him. "I've tried to find out," she answered. "I've spent a week trying. I've traced down the whereabouts of nearly every man within fifty miles on that afternoon. It wasn't as hard as you'd think. I'm sure of all but three men who matter. And only two of those ever had even an argument with my father. Only one of that pair ever had serious trouble with him."

"Who are the three?"

"Fred Snow, Phil Cable, and Jim Rosto."

Bill placed two of the three. Fred Snow was his father's cantankerous old ramrod. He'd always argued bitterly over the management of the outfit with Bob Ash, never meaning half of what he said. He had always stayed on beyond threats of leaving to do as fine a job as any man could. Bill ruled him out immediately, knowing that behind Snow's truculence lay a sincere and deep regard for Bob Ash. Phil Cable was president of the bank. Long ago he and Bob Ash had mutually agreed to have nothing to do with each other. Their trouble had come over Cable's refusal to loan Bill's father money when he was making his start. Old Bob Ash had always banked at Pinetop, a town thirty miles farther west. Bill couldn't place the third man and asked: "Who's Jim Rosto?"

"He's the one I meant when I mentioned serious trouble. It happened after you were gone, Bill. That fall your father was short of hands and hired Rosto, a stranger, for roundup. Your father caught him abusing a horse one day and had him thrown off the place. He made him buy the horse and take it with him, saying he'd ruined the animal. Rosto threatened to come after your father with a gun. Nothing came of it, and their feelings died down. Then, the following year, somcone talked Blaze Leslie into taking on a deputy. I think it was Ed Hoyt who decided it. He said Blaze was too old to be doing all the work and suggested Rosto for the job. They say he's been a good law officer."

"And you can't place Rosto on the afternoon of the murder?"

Linda shook her head, frowning thoughtfully. At length she gave an uneasy laugh: "It probably isn't important. Rosto left town the day before your father was killed, so he couldn't have done it. He took a rifle and enough food for two weeks and said he was going over into the Whetstones to hunt deer. They say he had that roan horse of his carrying twice as much as any man. . . ."

Bill stiffened. "A roan? Was that the horse my father made Rosto buy?"

Linda nodded, puzzled at his interruption.

Bill leaned closer to her. "That roan gelding with the split hind hoof?"

The girl thought a moment, then all at once nodded. "Yes, now that I think of it. I've noticed that split hoof. But why is that important?"

"I saw Rosto just before dark . . . up in the timber. He wasn't packing anything on his hull, and he was headed away from town."

Linda's look showed plainly that she was puzzled. "Then you think . . . ?"

"The first thing is to see Blaze and find out if Rosto's back from his hunt," Bill interrupted. "If he isn't, then we know he's holed up somewhere else, don't we?"

"Hiding?"

"You say he had a run-in with the old man. He left here the day before the murder, saying he was headed across into the Whetstones, sixty miles away. He was to be gone two weeks. Yet, with only a week gone, I see him riding in a blizzard, heading away from town and with no grub."

She saw what he meant now and said in an awed voice: "Then he didn't go across into the Whetstones?" Her eyes widened. "Bill! He could have done it!"

"Not so fast," he cautioned her. "He may have a reason for being back. If he does, Blaze will know about it. That's your job, to find out about Rosto from Blaze without his suspecting that you're after information."

Linda stood up. "I'll do it now."

"Careful," was Bill's last word to her.

* * *

Ten minutes later, when Linda returned to the shed, she found Bill asleep. She didn't have the heart to wake him. She knelt beside him and for long minutes looked down into his face, seeing that sleep had wiped out the bitterness and frustration that was, to her, the most terrible change these three years had made in him. Food and rest would fill out his gaunt, strong frame, but she wondered what it would take to rid him of the deeper wound these years had kept open deeply within him.

She went across to her room at the hotel and returned with a pair of blankets. She spread them over him. Her last gesture before turning down the lantern was to bend down and gently kiss him fully on the lips. She had to have that to seal the memory of what they had once meant to each other, to help her through the trouble she knew lay ahead. For Blaze Leslie wasn't expecting Jim Rosto back for another week.

III

The next day seemed endless to Linda. The blizzard was at its height, and the needle-sharp pennants of snow that rode the wind and cut at her face as she walked down the alley toward the shed at daylight seemed to fit her mood. She must be cautious in dealing with Bill, in telling him about Jim Rosto. For she understood the unbalanced desire for revenge that was driving him. She could be thankful for only one thing—his hatred was no longer centered on her father.

But when she sat in the shed, talking with him, she saw that she was powerless to head him off from trouble. When he heard that Rosto hadn't been seen in town for better than a week, he said ominously: "That means we've run onto something. I'll want a horse and some warm clothes and a gun, right away."

"Why, Bill?"

"I'm taking a look at that old Forked Lightning line shack up Snake Cañon. If he's hidin' out near where I saw him yesterday, it'll be there."

"But the storm, Bill!"

He smiled thinly. "It'll help. I won't be seen."

She had to give in to him finally and an hour later watched him ride away into the fog of snow. He rode a horse jaw-branded Sloping M, one of Tom Miles's regular string that Linda had taken from the feed barn. He wore a sheep-lined coat and Stetson that she had brought. Thonged low in a holster at his thigh was a gun, the one Linda had last night rammed in his back. It was her father's. She had carried it since the night he was arrested.

Seeing him ride out of sight, afraid at the thought she might never see him again, was only the start of a day crowded with disappointments for Linda. By three that afternoon, when she waited at the shed and saw Bill's tall figure coming back along the alley, her feeling of defeat was so complete that her thankfulness he was alive and safe couldn't outbalance it.

The first thing she saw as he stepped into the shed and closed the door was the small tear in the left shoulder of his jacket and the stain of blood that ringed it.

"Bill!" she cried. "Your arm!"

He moved his left arm stiffly, his eyes surface-glinted and hard. "He was up there, Linda. Waitin' down the cañon a quarter mile short of the shack. I'll go back again tonight. This time I won't give him as good a chance at me."

"Someone shot you, Bill?"

He nodded. "I was lucky. It's nothin' but a burn."

She insisted on looking at the wound. It was more serious than he had admitted, but the hole through the bunchy muscle that capped his shoulder was clean and he had bandaged it well.

Presently she was calm enough to tell him: "Bill, I have bad news. It wasn't Jim Rosto who shot at you. He rode into town this morning at eight o'clock! He's here now."

His hands reached up to take her by the shoulders. There was a wild light in his eyes. His grip was so vise-like, so hard, she gave an involuntary cry of pain. That brought back his reason. He took his hands away.

"I'm sorry, Linda," he said quietly. He was silent a long moment, then shrugged, and gave a long sigh. "Now what? I'd hoped we could take what we know to Blaze Leslie. I'd even give myself up to him if it'd make him wait a few days and look into this."

"We'll have to go to him tonight. He's away today, has been since early morning." She smiled without a trace of amusement in her eyes. "That's something else. People here were all so anxious to see Dad tried for the murder. Now their tempers have cooled off. They're remembering that they were his friends once. Blaze can't find anyone to act as hangman tomorrow morning. He's ridden over to San Juan to see if he can pick up a Mexican who'll do the job for ten dollars. He won't have any luck. They're friends of Dad's."

Had Bill been conscious of it, the caustic, bitter quality of her voice would have shown him how close she was to the breaking point. But something she had said took his attention so forcibly that he didn't recognize the near hysteria that lay behind her words.

"Blaze left town early this morning?" he said incredulously, turning something over in his mind. "Then *he* could have done it!"

"Done what?"

"Taken that shot at me up the cañon."

"Bill! Not Blaze!"

"Why not? Rosto was here, so someone else was up there near the line shack."

She said lifelessly, numbed by this new development: "Then we can't count on him for help."

He shot a sudden, seemingly irrelevant question: "Does Mart Schefflin still run his freight wagons through here?"

"Yes. But. . . ."

"And today's Thursday, isn't it, the day Schefflin's due?"

She nodded. "But in this weather he . . . "

"Mart Schefflin never let weather stop him, did he? If he hasn't already come through, this will work." She saw a new excitement and hope flash into his glance. "Linda, I'm going to get that job Blaze is offering!"

"You . . . you're going to hang Dad?" she said incredulously.

"I am! Only I promise you he won't hang."

"But . . . but how, Bill?"

"I don't quite know," he answered truthfully. "But I'm going out the trail beyond town and wait for Schefflin's wagon. I'll hop a ride. I'll be seen coming to town that way. I'll be a stranger. From there on I'll have to trust to luck."

"And if you're caught?" A deep concern for him was in her eyes.

He shrugged his wide shoulders. "I won't be," he drawled and wished he could believe he wouldn't.

Blaze Leslie stomped into his office at five that evening, his gray, longhorn mustache frosty and his narrow, hawkish nose blue with the cold. Jim Rosto sat in the chair at the desk back by the cell. His movement in coming up out of the chair was cat-like and lazy, its smoothness holding an economy of motion that seemed to fit the rest of his makeup, his dark and saturnine face, and his black eyes.

"Any luck?" he asked easily.

Blaze was surprised at seeing his deputy. He pulled off his sheepskin, threw it onto a nearby chair, and stepped over to the stove to warm his hands. "Not a damned bit," he growled in disgusted answer to Rosto's question. "How come you're back?"

"Game's all yarded up over in the Whetstones. Then this blow come along. I decided it'd be healthier under a roof."

From the cell at the back of the room Tom Miles's booming voice called: "You should have taken my word for it, Blaze! A hundred dollars couldn't hire a San Juan man to spring the trap under me. What'll you do now?"

Blaze stared back into the half light of the cell. "I wish to hell I knew, Tom," he said acidly.

He was a thoroughly beaten old man tonight, worn out, discouraged, hating his job. For thirty years he and Tom Miles had been friends, real friends. Circumstances he still couldn't trust called for him to be the witness to his friend's death at sunup tomorrow morning. All day he had thought of Tom and Linda and Bob Ash. Things like this just didn't happen. But they had. And, unless he could find another man, he himself would be pulling the trap that started Tom Miles on the ten-foot drop that would break his neck tomorrow morning.

Big, gruff, hearty Tom Miles was taking it the way Blaze had expected he would. When asked, Miles insisted on his innocence. But Blaze had never once detected a trace of fear in him. The rancher's stolid bearing was maddening at times. Blaze would have preferred a cringing, half-mad victim for his hangman's rope.

His dark thoughts were jerked rudely to the matter at hand as Rosto drawled in his toneless voice: "I think I've found your man, Blaze."

The old lawman wheeled on his deputy. "Who?" he demanded.

"A stranger," Rosto told him. "Rode in this afternoon on Schefflin's freight outfit. Tramp lookin' for a hand-out. He spent a dime for a beer at the Melodian and stuffed his mouth at the free lunch counter until Barney told him to lay off. Then he had the gall to ask Barney for a job."

Blaze only half heard what Rosto said. He was staring at Tom Miles, catching the smile that slowly came to the rancher's broad and rugged face.

"It looks like this is it, Tom," he said in apology.

Miles shrugged. "No one's blamin' you, Blaze. Go on over there and hire him."

Blaze sighed and nodded to Rosto. "Get him!"

The five-minute wait before Rosto came back with the stranger was a trying one for Blaze Leslie. He started to tell Miles how he'd hoped all along that something would save him. But words right now were pointless, more so because no shred of proof existed beyond Linda's loyal testimony at the trial. Blaze, like everyone else, believed that the girl had committed perjury to try to save her father.

His frowning glance sized up the stranger who came through the door ahead of Rosto. The scrubby beard hid a face that was lean and strong-looking. The man's thinned-out frame looked steely tough.

There was a sag in his left shoulder, a tear in that sleeve, high up toward the shoulder. But the beard and the unkempt hair, the red-rimmed brown eyes, and the outfit, much the worse for wear, convinced Blaze that he was looking at a saddle bum. No flicker of recognition showed in his eyes as he sized up Bill.

"Did you tell him, Rosto?" he said brusquely, and caught his deputy's negative shake of the head.

He eyed Bill so belligerently that Bill said: "Any law against ridin' a wagon in out of a storm, Sheriff? Or have you trumped up a charge against me?"

"No one's arrested you yet, stranger. What are you doin' here?"

Bill jerked his head to indicate Rosto. "Your understrapper said you wanted to see me."

"I don't mean that!" Blaze said curtly. "Why are you in town?"

Bill shrugged. "One town's as good as the next when it comes to lookin' for work."

"Any particular kind of work?"

"No. And I'm not particular." Bill smiled thinly at his twisting of the sheriff's words.

"I've got a job if you want it. Ten dollars for three minutes of work."

Bill frowned. "That's easy money. What's the catch?"

"We're hangin' a man tomorrow morning. We need a hangman."

Bill shook his head. "Uhn-uh, mister! Not me!"

"I'll make it fifteen dollars," Blaze said in a grating voice.

A shrewd look came to Bill's eyes. "How about fifty?"

"You go to hell!" Blaze snarled. Then he seemed

to think better of it. A long, gusty sigh escaped his narrow chest, and he said: "Fifty it is. Half now and half afterward." He took out his wallet, thumbed out five bills, and handed them across.

As he took the money, Bill looked hesitant. "I once saw a hangin' that turned out to be a stranglin'," he declared. "I don't aim to see this one the same kind. I'll take your job if you let me tie the knot myself to make sure it's right."

"Go ahead," Blaze said lifelessly, and stepped over to sit down in his chair. "Be here half an hour early in the mornin', at six."

"A man's fingers can't work in the cold at six in the mornin'," Bill asserted. "Get me the rope now and I'll take it with me tonight and tie it like it ought to be. Where's your gallows?"

Blaze nodded irritably to the street door. "Show him, Rosto. And buy him the rope."

As he and Rosto went out and along the walk, lowering their heads against the knifing wind, Bill said: "Salty old gent, ain't he?"

Rosto laughed softly. "Plenty. You're savin' him some gray hairs, stranger."

They made a stop at the hardware store where Rosto bought a twenty-foot length of new hemp rope. Two doors below they turned in at the feed barn and walked to the corral out back, where Rosto showed Bill the crude platform of new lumber two carpenters had nailed together that afternoon. The protruding beam that was used to hoist hay into the feed barn's loft was to be the gallows. The platform, twelve feet high and braced by scaffolding, was nailed to the side of the barn below the loft door and had a crude trap cut through it directly under the beam. The trap door was unfastened now, hanging downward on its shiny new hinges. Bill saw that it was sprung by a notched two-by-four pivoted in the platform.

Rosto pointed to the lever. "All you got to do is give it a good kick. Fifty bucks ought to be good pay if you don't happen to hurt your pet corn." He laughed.

"You act like this was a weddin'," Bill said dryly.

Rosto froze immediately. He held out the rope, drawling: "You ain't bein' paid for your talk, stranger. Remember that! Be here at six in the mornin'." With that he turned and walked back up the barn's runway and to the street.

Bill spent forty minutes that night working by the light of a lantern in the loft of the barn. Once he went down to borrow a tallow candle and a knife from the hostler, explaining that the rope would slip through the knot better if it was slick. But anyone watching would have seen that he had an added use for the tallow and that he used the knife for purposes other than trimming the end of the twelve windings of the knot.

At nine o'clock he was satisfied. He had secured the end of the rope to the beam and carefully measured its length so that he judged the loop would fit over Tom Miles's head as he stood on the platform and still leave eight or ten feet of slack. He ate a leisurely meal at Charley's place and smiled faintly after Charley had spent ten minutes talking to him without recognizing him.

Linda had said that she would be in the shed behind the jail at ten. He went there before the hour and found her waiting. As he entered the shed, he had a moment's panic at seeing a tall figure standing behind the girl's. Then he recognized Ed Hoyt.

"Ed wanted to speak to you, Bill," Linda said. "I have his word that he won't give you away."

Ed cleared his throat nervously. "This is a fool idea, Bill," he began. "If I'd been at the office this morning when Linda came to tell me what you were doing, I'd have stopped you. Instead of riding up there into the hills, you should have gone to Blaze. . . ."

"How much have you told him, Linda?" Bill cut in.

"All there was to tell, Bill. He wants to help."

Bill eyed Hoyt bleakly. "He wanted to help last night, too," he drawled.

"I was keyed up last night," Hoyt defended himself. "Didn't realize what I was doing. Linda has convinced me that her father's not guilty . . . not that I need convincing," he added as an afterthought. "What I want to know is what you plan for tomorrow morning."

"Why?"

"I'm one of the four men who's to be there. I could help."

"Who are the others?"

"Blaze, Jim Rosto, and Judge Morris."

Bill didn't show his relief. He had hoped that the witnesses to the hanging would be few. This meant that there would be, at the most, two men against him, Rosto and Blaze. Ed wouldn't interfere and old Judge Morris was physically harmless. He wished he could be sure of Blaze, but the sheriff's absence from town this morning had undermined the faith he'd always had in the lawman.

As he hesitated, Hoyt said once more: "How are you going to work it, Bill?"

"I don't know yet," Bill lied. He couldn't bring

himself to trust Ed Hoyt completely after last night's reception in the lawyer's office.

"But you must have some idea," Hoyt insisted.

"It all depends on what happens, who brings Miles up to the loft, who stays with him on the platform." Once that last statement was out, Bill immediately regretted it. No one but he and Linda had the right to know exactly what was going to happen.

He was irritated at Ed Hoyt's being here, for tonight would see the end of his and Linda's meetings alone. If he succeeded in getting her father away, he might never even see her again. She was promised to another man, and he begrudged sharing any of these last minutes with her.

"Linda, I want you to stay," he said sharply. "See you in the mornin', Ed."

There was an awkward moment's silence, one in which Ed Hoyt ignored the blunt invitation to leave. Then Linda said: "I'll go back to the hotel alone, Ed. It was good of you to come."

She and Bill stood silently a long quarter minute after the lawyer had gone out the door. Then Linda said: "You don't like him, do you, Bill?"

"I must've been too busy thinking about this other thing," he told her, neither admitting nor rejecting her accusation. Then, to change the subject, he said: "Here's one more thing for you to do. I'll want two horses on the street, as close to the feed barn as you can leave them. You might have Charley pack up some grub for us to take along."

"Where are you taking Dad?" Linda wasn't voicing the possibility that her father's escape might not succeed.

"To that line shack the first thing. After that . . . "
He shrugged.

That seemed to be all there was to say. The minutes dragged by for them both. Bill realized that his antagonism toward Ed Hoyt had brought a strained feeling between them. He was sorry to have hurt Linda's feelings yet was stubbornly unwilling to admit that he was wrong.

"It's late," she said finally. "I must be getting back." On impulse she reached out and took Bill's hand. "I . . . someday you may know how grateful I am, Bill."

"I'm doing it for myself as much as for you." He took her hand, clasped it, and took his hand away immediately.

"I know. But you are doing it, which is what matters. I wish things could have been different, Bill."

He tried to read a meaning into the words. He was finally sure it wasn't there. There was a tenderness in her glance, but that was gratitude alone.

She turned abruptly to the door and said—"Good bye, Bill."—and was gone.

He stayed on for another ten minutes in the shed, his thoughts bleak and empty. Beyond seeing Tom Miles free, he had no plans for the future. He might head for the border or go East to lose himself in one of the cities. He didn't much care.

Later, as he stretched out on the hay in the feed barn loft, he was an embittered man, alone, without hope, knowing that the last page in this chapter of his life was about to be closed, never to be opened again.

IV

In the hour between six and seven the next morning, while he waited in the loft for Blaze to appear, Bill Ash smoked cigarette after cigarette, telling himself that the tobacco tasted stale because of his own inner staleness. He wasn't hungry, although his stomach felt empty and dry. He was nervous. Three times he examined the six-gun he had thrust through the waistband of his pants. Three times he saw that the cylinder was loaded.

Relief came when he heard the sound of men coming slowly along the runway below. In another ten seconds Blaze Leslie's doggedly set face was rising into sight up the loft ladder.

Blaze was alone. "Let's get on with it," he said curtly.

They swung the hinged loft door outward and looked down into the feed barn's corral. Three men stood down there. Tom Miles's heavy, erect frame topped Ed Hoyt's by half a head, Judge Morris's by a full one. Ed and the judge were standing with their backs to the wind, stomping their feet calf-deep in the heavy blanket of snow, hands thrust deeply in overcoat pockets. Tom Miles seemed unaware of the wind or the snow but more interested in what was going on above.

His steady upward glance must have rubbed raw Blaze Leslie's nerve for, as Blaze let the rope with its noose fall out to hang from the beam, he grunted savagely: "To hell with this! I'm going down there and stay. I'll send one of the others up with the prisoner."

It was Jim Rosto who followed Tom Miles up the ladder into the loft half a minute after the sheriff had gone down. Miles's wrists were bound with a length of rawhide, and he no longer wore his flat-crowned Stetson. When Rosto took him by the arm and started leading him across to where Bill stood, alongside the open door, he jerked away. "I can make it alone, Rosto!" he said irritably.

For a moment Bill was afraid that Miles might throw himself from the loft door, preferring to die that way rather than at the end of a rope. But the rancher calmly followed him down the short ladder out of the loft door onto the platform. For about ten seconds they were alone there while Rosto was climbing down.

In that brief interval Bill stepped close to Miles, loosened the rawhide on his wrists, and said in a low voice: "Miles, I'm Bill Ash! Linda sent me. Don't ask why but, when you fall through that trap, stiffen your neck. When you hit the ground run through the barn for the street! You'll find two horses at the tie rail. Ride east out the street and cut north beyond town. I'll be right behind you!"

"What the hell's this all about?" Rosto's slow drawl said behind Bill.

Bill turned slowly to face the deputy. "I was askin'
if he wanted anything over his eyes."

For a long moment Bill thought the suspicion
would never leave the glance Rosto had focused on
Tom Miles. But finally the deputy's dark face broke
into a twisted smile.

"Him cover his eyes?" He laughed stiffly, cal-
lously. "Not Tom Miles." He nodded at the noose
swaying in the wind. "Do your stuff, stranger!"
Then, suddenly, his right hand pushed back his coat
and dipped to the holster at his thigh. He added
ominously: "I'm right here to see that you pull the
knot tight behind his ear!"

Bill tripped over the end of the two-by-four lever
as he stepped over to reach for the rope and pull up
the noose. The lever held and didn't let the trap
down. Rosto pushed Miles over onto the trap and
stood close while Bill lowered the noose over the
rancher's head, tightening the knot until it hugged
Miles's right ear.

As the knot closed, Rosto reached over Bill's
shoulder and ran his hand along the tallowed rope.
"What's the idea of this?" he growled suspiciously.

Bill knew then that Rosto had learned in some
way of the part he was playing here. The knowledge
settled over him in a wave of dread that finally
washed away to leave him cool and nerveless. He
turned to face Rosto. "That's so it'll tighten faster,"
he answered easily. "Are you doin' this, or am I?"

"By damn, I am!" Rosto snarled. He lifted the
heavy .45 from his holster and rocked it into line
with Bill. "Step back, stranger, and see how it's
done."

From below Blaze Leslie's voice rang out harshly: "What's goin' on up there?"

Bill glanced down. Blaze stood just below them in front of the scaffold, looking up. Ed Hoyt and the judge were farther out, their glances also directed above.

Then, before he quite knew what was happening, Rosto was muttering behind him: "You'll damn' soon find out!"

Bill wasn't ready for what happened with such startling suddenness. One moment he felt the platform quiver under the thrust of Rosto's boot as the deputy kicked the lever. The next, as he whirled around, he was in time to see Tom Miles shoot downward through the trap opening as the door banged solidly beneath the platform. The rope came taut, *whanged*, and curled upward loosely. Ed Hoyt's voice sounded in a shout of alarm from below. At that exact instant Rosto stepped over to line his gun down through the trap opening.

Bill lashed out hard, throwing all his weight behind his arm. His fist caught the deputy behind the ear a fraction of a second before the .45 exploded. Rosto sprawled downward to his knees. Bill jumped over him and through the opening. His breath caught as he plummeted down the twelve-foot drop, sweeping his coat aside to snatch the .38 from his belt.

His weight struck hard against the frozen ground. He went to his knees and fell sideways in a quick roll. Two guns exploded simultaneously, one from above, one from beyond the foot of the scaffold. The burn of a bullet scorched Bill's left thigh. As he rolled, he had a quick glimpse of Ed Hoyt, standing thirty feet away, a smoking gun in hand. Then his bewildered glance lifted to the trap opening on the scaffold above him. Rosto stood there, rocking his gun down on him.

Bill came to his feet, dodging aside as he threw a snap shot at Rosto. Their guns blended in a prolonged burst of sound. A geyser of snow puffed upward an inch out from Bill's right boot. He whirled in through the barn doorway and ran up along the passageway between the stalls. Halfway he wheeled in behind a bale of alfalfa and thumbed two swift shots out the maw of the back door. Ed Hoyt, running in through the doorway, stopped suddenly and lunged back out of it.

Bill came into the street in time to see three men running down the steps of the hotel, four doors beyond, and Tom Miles, astride a rangy claybank horse, swinging away from the tie rail. He ducked under the tie rail, pulling loose the reins of the other horse, a black. He vaulted into the saddle as three warning shots exploded hollowly from inside the barn. Bending low in the saddle, he wheeled the black out into the street and kicked hard at the animal's flanks with his spurless boots.

As they left the end of the street, swinging immediately north, Bill drew even with Tom Miles. They rode hard, silently, Bill looking back after they had gone on a full minute. He saw that the slanting cloud of wind-racing snow had already hidden the town from sight.

They put two more miles behind them before Bill tightened his reins to slow his black. Tom Miles pulled in and let Bill come alongside. The rancher's glance surveyed Bill critically an instant before his blunt face broke into a broad smile. "I wouldn't have given a nickel for my carcass when Rosto kicked open that trap," he said. "But my neck didn't even feel it. How did you work it, Ash?"

"Cut through most of the rope and tallowed it. The cut was hidden by the knot when I had it tight."

"Rosto knew what was up?"

Bill nodded soberly. "And Ed Hoyt gave me this." He ran his hand along his thigh, and his palm came away blood-smeared. When he saw the look of concern on Miles's face, he added: "I'm glad I got it. It proves a thing or two I've been wantin' to know."

"What?"

"Last night Ed Hoyt wanted to help me get you away. Linda was there. This morning he tried to cut me down. You figure it out, Tom."

He went on then, started briefly to tell the rancher what had happened in the last thirty-six hours. He was interrupted by a muted nearby hoof mutter riding the toneless scream of the wind. He kicked the black into a run as two shadowy figures loomed up out of the snow haze behind. A gun spoke once, its explosion whipped away by the rush of wind. The bullet made a concussion of air along Bill's cheek. He called—"Ride, Miles!"—and bent over in the saddle, cutting off to the left.

Linda had made a wise choice of horses, particularly in the claybank. Even with Tom Miles's heavy weight, the claybank more than matched the black's speed. Gradually those dim shadows behind faded from sight, and once more Bill and Miles were riding clear.

Bill purposely made a swing to the west, knowing

that the posse—if there were more than two men on their trail—would follow sign. Two more miles brought them to a broad and high shelf of rock. It stretched for a hundred yards to each side of them, its surface swept clean of snow by the wind. Bill right-angled to the north, thinking that the posse would waste perhaps a full minute in picking up the sign.

He rode point for the line shack in the cañon where the rifle had yesterday come so close to taking his life. He paid close attention to the horses now, slowing down out of a run to a stiff trot when the black gave signs of tiring. In these brief intervals he finished telling Tom Miles what had happened.

"We'll have a look at that shack and then go up the cañon and over the peaks," he finished.

"Over the peaks!" Miles blazed. "We're stayin' on here! I'm goin' to finish this thing!"

Bill smiled broadly. "I was hopin' you'd say that."

Today Bill rode straight up the narrow, twisting cañon, unmolested as he crossed the open stretch where the rifle had caught him yesterday. Beyond the widening in the high walls he caught the smell of burning cedar wood and knew again that his hunch on the line shack had been a shrewd one. A few seconds later he caught a glimpse of the so-droofed shack through the trees. A thin haze of blue smoke drifted lazily up out of the chimney.

They left their horses there and approached the shack by working in from tree to tree. When they were close, Bill motioned Miles to wait and made a quarter circle of the cabin before he went any closer. The snow deadened his footfalls as he crept up to the shack's single side window. He took off his Stetson and stood erect, looking in. He peered squarely across the small room at a blanketed figure lying on a bunk against the far wall. To his left, on the rear wall, was a huge stone fireplace where red coals glowed dully. He left the window, rounded the corner of the log wall to the front, and motioned Tom Miles to join him.

As Miles was coming up, Bill cocked his gun and reached out to pull down the rawhide latch string. He felt the latch raise and threw his weight against the door, wheeling in through it and lining his gun at the bunk. He stood there for two seconds, three, while Tom Miles came up behind him. The figure on the bunk didn't move. Bill walked over to the bunk and looked down into the graybearded face of the man lying there with closed eyes. Then, as his eyes adjusted to the light, he gasped and the gun fell from his hands. He went to his knees alongside the bunk and reached out, taking a rough hold on the sleeper's shoulders and shaking him hard. "Dad!" he cried. "Wake up! It's me, Bill! You're all right now!"

Tom Miles stared incredulously at the scene before him, Bill Ash there on his knees beside the bunk, his face drained of all color, calling hoarsely to his father. Finally, when Miles knew he wasn't looking at Bob Ash's ghost, he reached out and laid his hand on Bill's shoulder.

"Can't you see he's sick, Bill?" he said, his voice awed. "Take it easy."

Only then did Bill's reason return to him. He stared up dully at Miles, and tears came to his eyes. He breathed in a voice raised barely above a whisper: "He isn't dead, after all. He's alive."

It was Tom Miles who caught the hint of sound at the door. His big frame jerked around, stiffened. Slowly his hands came up to the level of his shoulders.

"Bill, we've got visitors," he said quietly.

Bill turned away from the bunk and glanced toward the door. Ed Hoyt stood, spraddle-legged, in the opening, a leveled .45 in each hand. Jim Rosto's dark face was peering in over Hoyt's shoulder. The lawyer caught Bill's look of utter confusion and laughed softly.

"I thought you'd have a last try at comin' up here," he drawled. "I won't miss this time, like I did yesterday."

Comprehension was slowly coming to Bill. He stayed where he was, there by the bunk, looking across at Hoyt for five long seconds. He said in a flat and toneless voice: "You're the one who framed me into Yuma?"

Hoyt nodded. "Linda was worth trying for," he said blandly.

Tom Miles caught his breath. "Damn your guts, Hoyt! You'll never marry her now!"

"No? And what's to stop me?"

"I will."

Hoyt laughed again. "They claim the dead rise up out of their graves. I've never believed it. But you can try, Miles."

As the rancher's face went slack under the threat of Hoyt's words, Bill said: "Why didn't you finish the job, Ed?" He nodded down to his father's inert shape in the bunk.

"A last detail that wasn't cleared up, Bill. You see, he still refuses to tell me where he put the copy of his will. I'm not even sure he signed it."

"You could have forged his signature to the one you have."

"Blaze saw my copy. He'd know it if he saw it again."

As Ed spoke, Bill had reached out to lay a hand on the top blanket in the bunk. As his hand moved, his father breathed a low moan. "What have you done to him?" Bill said sharply.

"Drugged him. Rosto brings him to once or twice a day and works on him. He's a stubborn man, Bill. We ripped off one of his thumbnails last night. That nearly did it. The other one comes off tonight. We'll break him in the end."

Ed Hoyt was getting an obvious satisfaction out of telling his story. Bill, staring into the twin muzzles of the pair of .45s, kept a firm check on the riot of hatred that was boiling in him. "How did you get him here?" he asked.

"Rosto brought him. In fact, it was Rosto who roped him off his horse that day up on the rim and pushed the horse over. I gambled on that, thinking no one was going to take the trouble digging through a hundred tons of rock to prove your father had . . ."

As Hoyt spoke, Bill's hand suddenly tightened on the blanket. He threw his body in a dive toward the door, swinging the blanket out over his shoulder and rolling into Tom Miles's legs. The blanket flew squarely at the lawyer, opening out. The double explosion of Ed Hoyt's guns beat the air of the room. Tom Miles fell heavily backward across Bill's legs, catching his breath with a groan that told Bill one of Hoyt's bullets had found a mark.

Bill's fury steadied to a cold nervelessness. His

right hand streaked out and closed on the gun he had dropped by the bunk two minutes ago. He swung the weapon up into line as the blanket dropped to the floor, two feet short of Hoyt. The lawyer's guns swiveled down. Bill's rocked into line, and he let his thumb slip from the hammer. The gun's solid pound traveled back into his shoulder. He saw Hoyt stagger backward, Rosto wheeling out of the door behind him. Then Hoyt's guns were slashing flame at him. A bullet gouged a splinter of wood from a floor plank. The splinter scratched Bill's face as he was shooting a second time, looking across the .45's sights.

Ed Hoyt coughed thickly as the bullet pounded into his chest. He went to his knees, his lips flecked with blood. Behind him Rosto stepped suddenly into the doorway, his guns swinging down. Bill was all at once aware that Tom Miles no longer lay across his legs. Then, suddenly, from behind him sailed the smoldering end of a cedar log. Rosto saw it coming squarely at him and dodged. That split-second hesitation of the deputy's was ended as Bill's gun exploded again. His bullet and the log end drove Rosto over backward, screaming. The deputy's body stiffened in a head-back arch. He lit that way in the snow beyond the door, his hands beating the ground wildly in a last convulsion that stiffened suddenly. Then his body went limp, and he lay without moving.

In the next hour much happened that Bill was never to forget. Blaze Leslie and half a dozen others rode up to the shack, their horses badly blown in the ride that had brought them up here following the sign of

Hoyt's and Rosto's ponies. Linda came later, in time to hear old Bob Ash tell what little he knew of what had happened during the last week. Strong coffee and a stiff jolt of whiskey had deadened the effects of the drug he had taken.

Bob Ash's glance clung fondly to his son as he told the men gathered around him: "Rosto met me up the trail on the rim that afternoon. Tied me and then drove that bay mare of mine over the drop-off. He brought me here. Hoyt came up that night, and they started work on me. Funny thing about that will he wanted me to sign. It was his idea from the first that you were guilty, Bill. I led him on to thinkin' I didn't have much use for you, just to see how far he'd go."

"But you've been here a long time. What's happened?" Bill asked.

His father shrugged and sighed wearily. "Nothin' much that I can remember," he said. "Two days ago I was ready to sign anything they gave me. But the drug was so strong I couldn't talk or even move my head. So it's Hoyt's own fault he didn't get away with this. Whoever gave him those knock-out drops didn't tell him how to use 'em."

It was another hour before Doc Selden rode up from town and took care of the flesh wound in Tom Miles's side and the bullet crease on Bill's thigh. As Selden strapped the bandage about Miles's ample waist, the rancher looked across at Bob Ash and at Bill and Linda sitting at the foot of the bunk.

His face reddened, and he said: "Bob, you're a cantankerous old mule, but so am I. Suppose we call it quits." He stepped over and thrust out his big hand.

Bill's father tightened his lips to hide a smile.

Then he frowned. "What good's shakin' hands? It'll take more'n that to make me forget you're so damn' bullheaded!"

Miles muttered a curse under his breath. "Supposin' I say I'll let Linda marry into your family."

"Don't know as I want her," Bob Ash insisted stubbornly.

"As if that mattered," Linda said, looking up at Bill. "Does it, Bill?"

He shook his head. Before he kissed her, he caught the sly wink his father gave Tom Miles.

Colt-Cure
for Woolly Fever

Jon Glidden came first to write Western fiction because of prompting from his brother, Frederick Dilley Glidden, who wrote Western fiction under the pseudonym Luke Short. During the Second World War, Jon Glidden served with the U.S. Strategic and Tactical Air Force in the United Kingdom. After the war, his novels were frequently serialized in *The Saturday Evening Post*. Elmer Kelton, a respected author of Western fiction, once observed that he had read all of Luke Short's stories and novels and that never once did one of the protagonists so much as crack a smile. Jon's model had always been Ernest Haycox among Western authors and he began in the serials and stories he wrote after the war to experiment with character and narrative technique in a fashion his brother never did. "Colt-Cure for Woolly Fever" is a humorous story, abandoning the reliance on serious circumstances, grim conflicts, and sober protagonists which had come to characterize so much of the Western fiction being written at the time, and thus setting the stage for the return of stories that stressed comedic elements, a quality that had become increasingly scarce in Western fiction written during the Depression and the war. This story first appeared in *Big-Book Western* (2/49).

I

They watched the stranger on the palomino coming down the pass trail, Jesúsita leaning languorously in the *cantina* doorway in one of those typically provocative attitudes that was Big Bill's reason for staying on here the last four days. Now, annoyed by the way she studied this oncoming rider so fixedly, he tongued his tobacco from one cheek to the other and spat expertly between his boots cocked on the *portal* wall. As the resulting puff of dust jumped from the roadway beyond, he observed sourly: "Never did see a runt forkin' that good a horse but what it was stole."

Jesúsita shrugged one shoulder, her dark eyes smoldering as they rocked around to him, then away again. He had decided from the first that this look betrayed her passion for him, although his several attempts at acting on that assumption had resulted only in the left side of his face being slapped hard.

So now, misinterpreting her glance as he usually did, he told her: "Say the word, *muchacha*, and that palomino's yours."

"Hah! The *gringo* talk beeg!" she said derisively, expansively, the firm yet gentle lines of her upper body standing out sharply with her quick intake of breath. "I no want the *caballo*, no notheeng from you!" As she turned in through the doors and left him, Big Bill chuckled so hard that his paunch bobbed, and he swore for the two hundred and thirty-seventh time that she would be his.

Everisto, her cousin, had been whittling at a knot on the step log, his ever drowsy glance on the rider who was coming into sight again from behind the spruce. Now, as he pried away a chip, he said: "Thees runt, you call heem. He wear the two beeg guns and he's not so leetle. The horse, she's too beeg to make heem look beeg."

Bill scowled, eyeing the rider intently. "He's a runt," was his considered opinion.

Shortly he and Everisto went indoors, both acting on the same impulse yet neither aware of its furtive quality. At such a remote place as this it was safest to show no curiosity over strangers. The *cantina*, with its offering of food and lodging, had thrived first because of Jesúsita's beauty and secondly because she, Everisto, and Papa who spent most of his hours asleep by the stove, all pretended to see nothing and know even less than nothing about the comings and goings along this trail. For the trail led from sheep country in the broad valley below to a vast cattle range the other side of the pass and, with the feeling strong between the two factions, the running of such an establishment called for a certain finesse.

So when the stranger got down from his palomino and stepped in through the swing doors some minutes later, Jesúsita was behind the bar rinsing lamp chimneys in hot, soapy water. Big Bill was bellied to the counter opposite her, sipping a glass of tequila. Everisto was doing something with a deck of cards at the room's only table, and Papa's unshaven chin was resting exactly where it usually did, on the front of his none too clean flannel shirt. His snoring only heightened the room's midday somnolence and struck a note in harmony with the buzzing of the flies at the windows.

"'Afternoon, folks," said the stranger pleasantly.

"*Buenas tardes, señor,*" murmured Jesúsita.

Her demure greeting was so at odds with that bolt-of-lightning quality Bill had so constantly sampled from her that Bill now pushed his paunch two inches from the bar and turned to eye the stranger. What he saw rocked him back on his run-over heels.

The man was, as Everisto had said, not small. Big Bill still topped his even six feet by a good four inches, but that wasn't what Bill noticed. Nor did he particularly note the stranger's blondness, or the lean handsome face. There was something else to displease his belligerent eye. The stranger's outfit was expensive. A nicely pressed black coat hung open over a fiery red shirt. The boots below clean waist overalls, also pressed, were fancy-stitched and polished till they shone. The pale gray hat was new, expensive, and didn't show any dust.

Despite all this it was three other items that had jolted Bill. Two were a matching pair of horn-handled Colts riding low along the stranger's flat thighs, the holsters thonged. The third was the ivory handle of a knife showing above the top of the polished right boot.

Big Bill took a certain pride in the armament he carried, and on his ability to use same. He'd done some carving on the cedar handle of his Navy Colt in the way of uniform notches representing certain luckless individuals who had had various and sundry fallings-out with him. A long time ago he'd worn a matching weapon, but an empty pocket and a smooth-tongued Mexican over in Las Cruces had whittled him down to being a one-gun man; he'd never bothered to replace the missing weapon. He always carried a big clasp knife in a pocket of his Levi's, one that would snap open, and on several occasions he had wielded it in what he invariably called self-defense—although his favorite close-in weapon was the neck end of a broken bottle.

He was big. He could use knife, gun, or bottle expertly. He'd never run across the man he couldn't lick. Nor had he ever missed an opportunity for showing himself the better man when meeting any individual who had the look of thinking himself able to take care of trouble. So now, after his deliberate inspection of the fancied-up stranger, Big Bill even more deliberately scowled and, disdaining any reply to the other's greeting, turned back to his glass.

"The handle's Matt, folks," the stranger said affably. "Who'll wet their whistle with me? Make it whiskey, *señorita*."

Everisto at once came over to the counter, grinning and nodding as he took the bottle the stranger passed him and filled his glass. "*Gracias, señor, gracias*," he said.

The stranger offered Big Bill the bottle then, and Bill said with a surly snarl: "I pass."

"Every man to his own taste," Matt drawled.

If he hadn't turned his back on Big Bill just then, the thing might have been settled sooner. All Bill could think of to do was to glower at Jesúsita, which only made the smile she was giving the stranger more radiant.

This Matt took up his glass now, saying—"To all beautiful women."—and drank the toast with his pale blue, laughing eyes taking in Jesúsita's dark loveliness.

Afterward he tossed a silver dollar to the counter, and Jesúsita made change, a half dollar and two dimes. Whereupon the stranger stared down at the coins. "You didn't take out enough, miss."

She made a pretty play of hands and shoulders in telling him: "Fifteen cents the dreenk, señor."

"Cheap," he said.

Big Bill had suddenly had enough of this folderol. He pounded the bar loudly. "Sheep?" he roared. "What about sheep?" He wheeled with the clumsiness of a grizzly to throw what tequila remained in his glass squarely into the stranger's eyes.

If he hadn't thought to draw his .44 at the same time, he wouldn't have lived to add his bit to the lurid history of Chiricahua County. For, although nearly blinded, Matt's right hand dropped to his Colt so fast the eye could scarcely follow.

The hammer click of Bill's weapon was all that stopped the stranger's draw. Smiling broadly then, the tequila dripping from his chin, Matt lifted his empty hand carefully and laid it palm down on the bar. Jesúsita picked that moment to burst into a torrent of Spanish, which dealt plainly with the obscurity of Big Bill's ancestry.

Presently, when he had blinked his eyes clear of the fiery liquid, Matt politely raised a hand and motioned Jesúsita to silence. Then he looked up at Bill, who held the Colt still lined at the middle button on his shirt. "Just what did I say to upset you, friend?"

"Sheep! What the hell else?" Bill roared, Jesúsita's tongue-lashing having blunted the sharp edge of his temper not at all. "The only sheepman I drink alongside is a dead one!"

"Now you've got me wrong," Matt replied smoothly. "Fact is, I can't stand the stink of sheep. So tell the *señorita* you're sorry. Then you can put that hog-leg away and fill your glass again. It's my treat."

"Sorry for what?" Bill's roar hadn't diminished. "Turn yourself around and keep them hands where they are!"

For a fraction of a second he caught the wintry look in the stranger's eyes and should have been warned by it. But the chip he'd put on his shoulder was too big to let fall now, and, reaching out roughly and grabbing this Matt by the arm, he pushed him around. Then, ramming the muzzle of his Colt in at the man's spine—he had a second warning there, for the muscles along that back were like oak—he relieved him of his pair of matched .45s.

Using his own weapon to push the stranger away from him, he bellowed: "Next time you figure to drink alongside a cattleman, bring your big brother with you, runt!" And with that he headed for the doors, satisfied that when Jesúsita had time to consider the last few moments she would see him for what he was—a brave and strong man.

He carried Matt's two guns by their trigger guards hanging from his big left index finger, and, as he came up on the doors, he reached out with his other hand to push them aside. That hand was touching the wood when he felt what he thought was a fly touch his ear. A wing of brightly reflected sunlight flashed past his eye. There came a thrumming sound and the door stirred slightly away from his hand. A split second later he saw the ivory-handled knife that had grazed his ear quivering in the door panel. Behind him he caught the sound of something thudding solidly against the bar.

"Now hold on," came Matt's mild drawl.

The color drained from Big Bill's face. He stood there rigidly, his back still to the room. He was remembering the shotgun Jesúsita always kept under the bar, which would account for the sound he had just heard, and he was imagining its front bead centering the small of his back. So he stood rooted as he was, staring at the knife and blinking away a sudden flow of perspiration from his forehead that trickled down into his eyes and off the end of his bulbous nose.

"You forgot to tell the *señorita* you're sorry, friend," Matt told him.

Big Bill thought to drop the three guns then and they clumped solidly to the hard-packed earth floor as he tried to speak, but couldn't. He swallowed to rid his throat of its cottony dryness, and then, strictly because he was as afraid as he'd ever been, he said meekly, haltingly: "I . . . I reckon I done wrong, *muchacha*."

"Now that's a real nice sentiment," Matt North told him. "You can trot along if you feel like it."

Big Bill shouldered out through the doors and was gone.

"Ornery cuss, eh?" Matt said, setting the bottle back on the bar. He had been holding it ready in case his swift knife throw hadn't completely awed the big man, and it was its accidental banging against the counter that had made Big Bill think of the shotgun.

"Beel, she's the beeg peeg!" Jesúsita sighed with relief at the relaxing of the tension, and now her eyes flashed with loathing. "He come here three, four day ago. He say to me . . . '*Muchacha*, you and me go to see priest an' get married, no? You leave thees place w'ere the mens she's always trying to kees you and make the love. W'at about eet, Jesúsita?' An' I tell heem no man make the love to me for I heet and bite if she do. So Beeg Beel, he laugh and peench me on the arm. I heet heem. Then he peench me other places, and I heet heem some more. But still she theenk thees is the way I make the love to heem, so he 'ang 'round. I take hees monee and let heem make the beeg eyes. W'at I care?"

Matt was only vaguely aware of what she had been saying, so entranced was he by the play of her eyes and graceful, quick motions of her hands. He knew he was staring at her calf-eyed, but didn't care. Now he let out a gusty breath. "Sita, you're the prettiest thing I ever laid eyes on!"

She liked that. Everisto, watching, could hardly believe his eyes, for he knew she had been telling the truth about not tolerating the advances of men customers. Yet here she was, smiling in confusion, obviously liking this stranger's words.

"Tha's wot Beel say, 'You beauteeful, *muchacha*,'" Jesúsita put in hastily now. "So w'en he say eet, I heet heem. Like thees."

Before Matt could dodge, she leaned over the counter and slapped him across the face so hard his head rocked to the side. But then instantly there was a look of contrition in her eyes and she was crying: "Oh, *señor*, I no mean that!" Just as quickly as she'd moved a moment ago, she now leaned closer to him and, patting his cheek, murmured, "¡*Pobrecito!* For a meenute I theenk you Beel. I too sorry, *Señor* Matt!"

"Didn't hurt a bit, *señorita*." Matt was rubbing his cheek. "Not a bit."

"Matt," she sighed, elbows on the counter, her face close to his and her eyes ever so soft. "That's one nice 'andle. Matt. Veree nice."

She had such a gone look right then that Matt gulped and reached for the bottle. He poured himself a drink and downed it at one swallow, for he was a slow hand with the opposite sex and this girl with the flashing eyes was sweeping him off his feet. He wanted to touch her, maybe even try a kiss. Instead he blurted out: "Couldn't we . . . that is, couldn't you and me go down to town some night and kick up our heels at a dance, Sita?"

She drew away, wide-eyed in alarm. "No, no! Papa, he take the belt and wheep." Unashamedly her hand went to her backside. "You come see me 'ere, Matt. We seet on the *portal* one night teel Papa asleep, no?"

"Sure." Matt gulped. "Sure thing."

"But not in the town," Jesúsita said, wrinkling her

nose. "The town, she steenk of cheep. Once it was *differente*. W'en I the leetle girl everyone, they 'appy. Papa, 'e was the *vaquero* then. He rope the beeg steer and tweest 'is tail an' he wear the wot you call bool-'ide pants. But then the cheep mans come in and weeth the gons they fight and drive the cattlemans out. So now Papa, he 'ave the seekness of the 'eart and he seet there all day dreaming of w'en 'e was the wan fine *vaquero* and ron the cattle."

Matt's look had turned grave and now he glanced at Papa in the chair by the stove and nodded. "I've heard about your ruckus here. No one's tried to push these sheep-lovers out of the valley since then?"

"They always talking." She lifted her shoulders eloquently. "But no one, he do notheeng. Beel, he say he go down to rob the bank because he hate the cheep man. But all she do ees talk beeg. Beeg Weend, I call heem. He got the beeg talk from the beeg belly."

Matt's glance went to the doors. "So Bill would like to bust open the bank, eh?"

"He like to fine. But he no have w'at you call the gotts."

"Guts."

"Tha's w'at I say, Matt. The gotts."

Matt's glance was still on the doors and now he drawled absent-mindedly: "Maybe Bill and I could get along." He moved on over from the bar then and picked up the guns, holstering his own pair and ramming Bill's through the belt of his Levi's.

He was standing there, looking out over the doors when Jesúsita cried quickly in alarm: "You no go out there, Matt! Beel, he keel you. He the wan toff *hombre!* He got the rifle on 'is 'orse."

Matt's lean face broke into a smile. "So I see. He's got the rifle right enough. But not his horse. He's gettin' onto Whitey."

"W'itey?"

"My palomino."

His smile still holding, he turned and came back to the bar. He picked up the bottle and laid two silver dollars on the counter, telling her: "This Bill and I are going to make some medicine, Sita."

Then, as he went to the doors again, she cried: "Matt, stay weeth me!" But he only shook his head and stepped out onto the *portal*.

At that moment Big Bill, astride the palomino, was turning out from the *cantina*'s tie rail. He saw Matt and, his look turning ugly, leveled the .30-30 Winchester he had been holding with stock cradled against his thigh.

"Back in there, runt!" he called hoarsely, trying to quiet the palomino's head tossing and nervous side-stepping.

Matt's smile only widened and for several seconds he watched the muzzle of Bill's rifle bob up and down to the nervous pitching of the animal. Then abruptly he whistled. At that sound the palomino suddenly reared high on hind legs, and Bill, dropping the carbine and reaching for the horn a split second too late, slid heavily down over the animal's rump and hit the ground with a pained grunt. The palomino at once quieted and walked on past the rail and in under the *portal* to rub his nose fondly along Matt's arm.

There was a point beyond which Matt didn't want to humiliate the big man, so he wasn't smiling now. "Whitey's a handful, Bill. Should've warned you. That's a trick I taught him."

Big Bill's face was dark with an apoplectic look and his furious glance went to the carbine. But it was too far beyond his reach to give him a chance against even an average draw. So he picked his hat out of the road, beat the dust from it, clamped it on his head, and heaved his vast hulk erect. Matt sauntered on out and, drawing Bill's .44, held it out to him butt foremost. At the same time he hefted the bottle in his other hand. "Let's you and me pick a spot of shade and wash the dust out of our windpipes. I got something to talk over with you."

Bill's angry glance became uncertain now. With a downlipped sneer he took his gun and stood glowering down on the smaller man, as though undecided as to what to do next. But something in Matt's eyes made him finally holster the weapon. Then, grudgingly, he accepted the bottle as Matt uncorked it and offered it.

They each took a long pull at the bottle, and then Matt led the way to the shady side of the *cantina*. There he sat with his back to the wall, putting the bottle between them as Bill joined him. Bill was still studying him suspiciously as Matt said: "The girl in there says you got a notion to bust open the bank down below. Now you and me got something in common."

"What?" Bill growled.

"Hatin' sheep," Matt told him. "And wantin' to lay hands on some easy sheep money."

Bill's frown faded before a slow surprise. "Well, I . . . that is, you might say I got my eye on that there bank," he admitted haltingly.

"Think the two of us together could pull the thing off?" Bill blinked, obviously caught unawares. As he hesitated, Matt continued: " 'Course, if you think it's too risky. . . ."

"Who the hell said I thought that?"

Bill had swallowed his tobacco when he had sat so suddenly there in the road, and now he took a plug of the weed from a shirt pocket, needing time to think. He bit off a generous hunk, then handed it to Matt. After Matt had taken his bite, they silently passed the bottle between them again. Finally Bill said: "Ain't nothin' to be afraid of. Except maybe for that tin safe bein' so full of money two men couldn't haul it all away."

"We could make two trips," Matt said blandly, making Bill blink again and wonder just what this stranger's nerves were made of.

"Here's the way she looks to me," Bill went on, groping his way through his slow thoughts and trying to remember how the bank had looked on his trip down to Pleasantville day before yesterday in Jesúsita's buckboard. "They've ordered a new safe shipped in. But she ain't here yet, which has caught 'em with their galluses down. They've got the back wall of the bank knocked out with a hole big enough to drive a team through. So they can get the new safe in when she comes. The thing's boarded over now and that sheep-lovin' sheriff, Clyde Case, takes turns with his deputy day and night watchin' to see no one comes along with a hammer and breaks in. Must be close to thirty or forty thousand in the old safe."

"How much of a job will it be to open the thing?"

Big Bill laughed so hard his paunch shook. He made another pass at the bottle before he answered: "I got a knife in my pocket'll do the job slick as a whistle."

"Then let's do it tonight."

Matt's words made Bill sit straighter. "Tonight?" he echoed. "I . . . well, y'see, I was thinkin' me and Jesúsita might go for a walk up toward the pass tonight."

"Now that's a shame," Matt said innocently. "Here I thought you might help."

Things were moving too fast for Bill. "Hadn't we ought to go down there and look the thing over first? You, I mean."

Matt nodded. "Just what I was thinkin'. Give me the rest of the afternoon and I'll meet you wherever you say. Let the girl wait, Bill."

The big man sighed, for the way Matt talked made the thing sound easy. Then he remembered something and, scowling at Matt, said: "You looked pretty sweet on her in there."

Matt's wide grin held a guilty look. "Sure. I always give 'em a try, Bill. But if she's yours, I'll lay off."

"She damn' well is!" Bill flared. "You and me got to get that straight if we're sidin' each other."

"That's easy," Matt said. He held out his hand. "So long as we're partners we don't mix our women. OK?"

Bill nodded. He was smiling for the first time as he wrapped his big fist around Matt's and shook it.

II

The men and women in Pleasantville who observed Matt's arrival were unanimous in their reactions. Most of the men wished they could own the horse and most of the women would have given anything to own the man, so by the time he turned in at the livery corral to leave the palomino, more than a few of the folks were already curious about him.

He went straight to the hotel, his bedroll slung over his shoulder, and there were half a dozen townsmen in the lobby to overhear him tell the clerk as he signed the book: "The best room you got, friend. With a bath."

"Mister, there ain't a foot o' plumbin' on the premises."

Matt's brows lifted in polite surprise. "No? Well, maybe I'll build a hotel of my own with some. This is sure a wore-out-lookin' settlement, friend. Give me the best you got."

Once he and the clerk had climbed the stairs from the lobby, the several men who had overheard these remarks hastened to discuss them, quickly forgetting their anger over the slighting way he had spoken of the town. One of the group went to the desk for a look at the register and shortly rejoined the others to say: "Calls himself North . . . Matthew V. North."

They made several conjectures on the stranger's identity, most of which were based on his asking for a bath and his look of affluence, and by the time Matt came down the stairs again they were very respectful in the way they answered his casual nod.

Matt's next stop along the street was at a shack with a shingle hanging over its door bearing the legend: **LAND FOR SALE. RANCH AND TOWN PROPERTIES.** He was in there a good twenty minutes, and, as soon as he left, crossing over to the bank, Mayor Williams and two other men who had been in the hotel lobby went into the shack to ask what had gone on.

"Plenty," they were told. "North took out options on every outfit we got for sale, includin' Ives's place. And on those eight lots down the street where we give up buildin' the new opera house."

"God in heaven," the mayor breathed. "Who is he?"

"Calls himself North, Matthew. . . ."

"We know that! But where's he from?"

"He didn't say and I didn't ask. One thing, though. He ain't so taken with the idea of runnin' sheep." The mayor and his companions looked at each other as their informant shortly continued: "I told him, if he was settlin' here, it'd be sheep or nothin'. He just looked at me sort of queer, like I needed a haircut maybe or a shave. Said he'd think it over, that he wanted to invest around a hundred thousand in good grass and town lots and. . . "

"A hundred thousand?" one of the others whispered. Then, finding his voice, he said quickly: "Let's get on over and see Caleb. He may know more about North."

But two minutes later Caleb West, president of the bank, couldn't add much to what they already knew of the stranger—except that he'd refused to bank any money until the present safe was replaced by an adequate vault.

"Vault?" the mayor said. "You didn't order no vault, Caleb."

"Who said I did?" Caleb countered in irritation. "But I can order one in place of the new safe, can't I? Fact is, I already got a man ridin' across to Junction to send a telegram about it."

While they were speculating further on the importance of this Matthew North's arrival, and on what his money would do for the town, Sheriff Clyde Case joined them and was presently inserting a new note into their conversation as he observed: "You boys better let me take a look at my dodgers before you get so steamed up over this bird."

"Clyde, for the love of the good Lord, why spoil our fun?" the banker asked. "You'd suspect your grandmother of bein' a squaw woman if she hadn't lived long enough to let you have a good look at her." He, like the rest, had little patience with the sheriff for the reason that Case had twelve years ago kept plenty far out of the way of flying lead during the war with the cattlemen.

"You go look through your dodgers, Clyde," the mayor said. "But danged if we'll let you insult this gentleman and scare him off."

So Case, grumbling about their ingratitude when he was only looking after their best interests, left the

bank and went to his office and stubbornly set about
going through his disorderly collection of reward
notices. He was halfway through the stack when
Matt came in off the walk, saying pleasantly: "'Afternoon, Sheriff. Have a cigar?"

Clyde had a guilty, surprised look as he got out of
his chair and took the cigar. "Thanks, Mister
North," he said respectfully. "I been hearin' about
you. Have my chair."

But Matt was noticing the dodgers and, now taking his own cigar from his mouth and nodding
down to the desk, said: "That's a funny thing. I
dropped in here for this very reason, Sheriff. To look
through your Wanted notices."

Clyde Case's weasel-eyed glance turned impas-
sive. He ran a thumb along his tobacco-yellowed
brown mustache, put the cigar in his mouth, and
started chewing it as he asked off-handedly:
"Lookin' for one in particular?"

"Sure am." Matt watched the lawman's jaws
working at the cigar. He regretted having given
Case the smoke now, for he had just spent one of
his last few dollars on eight fine cigars and he could
already see that this one was wasted. So, as he
sighed his disappointment, he told Case: "On the
way over here I ran onto a jasper that had a mean
pair of ears. Big as a house, a front on him like a
barrel. A nose too big for his face and they called
him Bill."

"Big Bill!" Case nearly choked on the cigar. He
got red in the face and his voice was trembling when
he went on: "That yellow-livered coyote! Mean as a
grizzly and twice as dangerous. Tell me where I can

find him and I'll blow a hole through his back. His *back*, mind you! He's wanted on any one of ten counts that'll hang him."

"Now hold on," Matt said mildly. "Don't get so aforesaid. For all I know this Big Bill may be three hundred miles from here by now. On the other hand, he was headed this way."

"The hell you say!" Case stepped quickly to the door, stuck his head out, and bawled: "Avery! Get across here!"

"What's up?" Matt asked.

"Avery's my deputy," Case told him, his look worried as he chewed the cigar furiously. "Mister North, you got much ready cash on you?"

Matt frowned. "Would a couple thousand be what you call ready?"

The sheriff's eyes bugged open. "Ready and then some! Well, you hide that there money *pronto!* If Big Bill breezes through here and finds there's a well-heeled stranger in town, he'll take every damn' nickel you got."

"No one takes my nickels," Matt drawled.

"You pay attention to what I'm tellin' you!" said the lawman excitedly. He gave a start as the door opened. But when he saw who it was, a tow-headed youth who was working at his teeth with a splinter of wood, he said officiously: "Avery, go to the hardware and get every shotgun Blaine's got in the place. Hand 'em out to the best shots. Beginnin' at dark, we're goin' to have twenty armed men prowlin' this street."

"How come?" Avery wanted to know.

"How come! Big Bill's been seen close to here and for all we know he . . . " The sheriff's words broke off, for he was speaking at an empty door. Avery had already left, on the run.

"Why get so het up?" Matt asked. "If the law gets this spooky over one lone wolf, maybe I ought to look for some other place to settle."

"Mister North, you got us wrong," Clyde hastened to assure him. And for the next several minutes he did his best to convince Matt that Pleasantville was exactly what the name would indicate, a pleasant place to live, safe as the inside of a church at meeting time, the best climate in the world, the best of everything. "Take grass, for instance," he ended by saying. "I hear you're of a mind to buy some land. Well, sir, there ain't an animal ever lived was so sick that a week on this grass wouldn't cure him. It's plumb past believin', but we never lose a head of anything in this valley except for butcherin' or some pet critter now and then dyin' of old age. Ever see anything to beat the looks of them sheep you passed on the way in?"

"I kind of hoped to run cattle, Sheriff."

Case stiffened, started to look angry, decided for private reasons not to. He shook his head. "Nope, sheep's all we run here. The time was, ten or twelve years ago, when they ran cattle. Them damn' critters near ruined the valley. You know how cattle are, pullin' the grass up by the roots and . . . "

"I always thought it was the other way around."

"No, sir! You take my word for it, neighbor, it's cattle and not sheep that ruin the range. So," the lawman went on, deciding he had proven his point, "a few of us up and decide we'll save what's left. For a week or two it was nip and tuck, the lead flyin' so thick you didn't dare set foot outdoors by day. Then finally we drove Matt Rivers and his gang . . . "

"Did you say Matt Rivers?"

The sheriff nodded. "Matt Rivers. He was leader of them cattlemen. Set up a lot like you, come to think of it. Your build, them big shoulders and all. And pale hair like yours."

"That's funny," Matt drawled. "Matt's my first name, too. We got a parcel of Rivers in one branch of our family and for a minute here I was thinkin' this man you mention might be some kin. But I reckon not."

"Probably not or you'd have heard of him before now. We chased him and his bunch over the pass and later we heard he had died from a chunk of lead through his middle. They tell me you've taken out an option to buy Ives's place, among others. That's the old Rivers's layout, the old Anvil brand."

"Y'don't say!"

"Yep. And a right nice layout it is, too. Ives, he wants to sell on account of bein' ready to retire. He's made a big killin' up there on that Anvil grass with all the water and meadow he's got and he'll sell for the right price. Thirty thousand, they say."

Matt nodded. "That's the price quoted to me."

The sheriff had become quite affable and now slapped Matt on the back, saying: "Well, sir, you couldn't find a better place at a better price. Take it before Ives changes his mind. And try sheep, Mister North. You can't go wrong on a wool crop."

"I'll think it over." Matt lifted a hand, said—"See you later, Sheriff."—and left.

He hadn't gone twenty steps when a portly individual standing at the walk's edge below the jail stopped him. "Mister North, let me introduce myself. I'm Mayor Williams." He took Matt's hand and pumped it hard, adding affably: "Some of the boys are hoisting one across in the Nugget, since it's the shank of the day. We'd admire to have you join us."

"Now that's real white of you," Matt said and, the mayor linking an arm in his, let himself be led across the street to a saloon.

III

During the hour he spent in very pleasant company in the Nugget, he several times put a hand in his near-empty pocket, announcing that the next round of drinks was his. But each time his offer brought a storm of protest, for several others had joined the gathering and new money was anything but scarce. Several of these last joiners were carrying shotguns—the ones the sheriff had ordered handed out at the hardware store—and, as they took their drinks, they passed the guns across the bar to the apron for safekeeping so that by the real shank of the evening, suppertime, the backbar looked like a gun case with its array of new and shiny weapons.

When the subject of eating presented itself, Matt was invited to dine with several of the town's most eminent citizens. He accepted graciously. The meal was larded with much boisterous whiskey-livened talk and consumed an hour and a half. Toward the end of it Matt was beginning to feel uneasy and kept glancing at the clock over the counter.

Finally, when it appeared that the evening had only begun, he rose from his chair and announced: "Gents, I thank you for one fine mess of food. But there's work to be done. If this curly wolf, Big Bill, is really due to shoot up the town tonight, let's get set for him."

"Why, I'd almost forgot Big Bill," the mayor said. He wasn't too steady on his feet as he rose to stand alongside Matt, who noticed him licking his lips and wondered at the reason until the mayor said loudly to the others: "Boys, the nights are gettin' right chill. What say we get ourselves a bottle or two to help us last till mornin'?"

There was a general agreement. Someone reminded the assemblage that they had left their guns at the Nugget, so they straggled out and across the street, a man on either side of the newcomer and both calling him "Matt" now instead of "Mister North".

When they were finally gathered in front of the Nugget, armed with their shotguns and a quart bottle for every other man, the mayor spoke for all of them in asking: "Where do you want us, Matt?"

This matter took some thought and for a moment Matt didn't answer. Then finally he said: "I don't know the town, boys. Let the sheriff decide."

"Where the hell is Clyde?" someone asked.

"Out behind the bank watchin' the alley, ain't he?"

"Someone go get him."

"Tell you what," Matt inserted, knowing it was well past the hour he had set for meeting Big Bill. "I'd like to wander on out the street and look it over, get the lay of the land. While you're gettin' the sheriff, I'll roam about by myself a minute or two."

Mayor Williams wanted to come with him but Matt took him aside and said quietly: "Better stay with the bunch. They're likkered up and need watchin'. Keep your eye on them. I'll be right back."

Williams was swaying a little and had to stand, spraddle-legged, to keep his balance. He, like the others, had had a lot to drink. Now he was licking his lips again, wanting more as he said: "Y'know, Matt, I think Clyde thought this Big Bill business up as a joke on us. Whyn't we all just go in there, set ourselves down, and enjoy a few more drinks and some cigars? Maybe a game of draw?"

"It wasn't Clyde thought it up, it was me."

"So it was, so it was," Williams grumbled. "Well, you get on and I'll keep an eye on this bunch."

Matt went on before the mayor could change his mind. Half a minute's walk brought him abreast the big livery corral. The street was dark here, and after a look both ways along the walks he climbed the gate and hurried on toward the back of the big enclosure, the shadowy shapes of several horses drifting out of his way in the darkness ahead. He found that his steps were slightly uncertain and wished now he hadn't taken so many drinks.

He was coming up on the spidery black silhouette of the windmill beyond the back rails when he remembered the big, log watering trough. A sigh of relief escaped him as he took off his hat and coat and, laying them aside, dipped his head into the cold water brimming in the trough. Then, for some strange reason, he got to thinking of Sita and just stood there for a minute or two.

He was scrubbing his face again presently, feeling his senses steadying under the chill bite of the water, when a sound made him wheel around. Instinctively in one smooth flow of motion he palmed the Colt from his right thigh, softly asking: "Who is it?"

"Me," answered a deep-toned voice—Big Bill's. "Where you been all this time?"

"Layin' the way for an easy job," Matt answered. He dropped the Colt back into its scabbard, pulling out the tails of his shirt and using them to dry his head. Then, without giving Bill a chance to complain further, he said: "Now here's what we do." And he went on to explain exactly what was to happen. He ended half a minute's steady talk by saying: "So it'll be a cinch. Remember, there'll be a loose board. When I light my cigar, you go in that way. Be quiet while you're inside and wait in there till I come after you. Where the hell's all the gunny sacks?"

"Tied to my hull."

"Then we're all set, Bill. Give me fifteen minutes."

But something was bothering Big Bill, for he made no move to walk away and shortly he said in a voice that grated: "One man double-crossed me once. I drop by the cemetery at Socorro every now and then to take flowers off his grave. His family leaves 'em."

"That's not the way you'd want your grave treated, Bill."

"You mind this, now," Bill growled, in no mood for nonsense. "I get my half . . . no matter what."

"And see that I get mine," Matt said. "After all, I'm leaving the business of the split to you."

Without another word, Bill turned and walked away in the darkness.

IV

Mayor Williams and four men were set to watch the lower end of the street while another group stationed themselves along the stretch of awninged walk above the hardware store. "Me, I'll go give the sheriff a hand," Matt offered. No one questioned his statement. It was as easy as that. So he went on down to the bank.

Taking the narrow passageway alongside the bank, he was careful to be loudly whistling a tune, trusting Clyde Case's steadiness not at all.

"Who the hell's makin' so much noise?" came the sheriff's sharp query as Matt stepped out of the back end of the passageway.

"Me, Sheriff. How do things look?"

"Oh, you, Mister North." Case came up out of the shadows. "They don't look so good if you ask me."

"Why not?"

"We need more men back here."

"You and me can handle our end," Matt assured him.

That seemed to quiet the lawman's jumpy nerves somewhat and for a minute or two they talked in low voices, Matt telling Case how the townsmen had distributed themselves along the street. Then, presently, Matt asked: "How easy would it be for a man to break into the bank?"

"How easy is it for a kid to fight his way into a sack of candy?"

Matt whistled softly. "Y'don't say. Let's take a look."

Case led the way on along the bank's back wall and after several steps they came up on a portion of the wall that showed a lighter shadow. "If that ain't a pretty sight!" the lawman said disgustedly.

It wasn't very strong, Matt could see, even in this poor light. A rectangular hole about as tall as he was and twice as wide had been boarded up. He stepped in close to it, swung a boot back, and kicked hard at one of the wide boards. "Flimsy, eh?"

"Don't!" Case snapped worriedly. "Hell, you'll kick the whole thing loose."

He was more right than he imagined. For Matt had seen the base of that one board swing out, the nails pulled free under his kick. Here was the first thing of the several he had mentioned to Big Bill already accomplished. Now for the second, he told himself as he said: "Let's take a look up at the other end."

He and Case walked on to the far end of the wall. Matt took a cigar, his last, from the pocket of his coat. "What's up in there?" he asked, nodding up a passageway even narrower than the one he had traveled from the street.

"Nothin'." Case stepped into the passageway,

adding: "Nothin' but a rain barrel in here you got to watch out for. Right here."

"Glad to know about it." Matt wiped a match alight along the seat of his pants and, as it flared, held it out openly and unshielded by his hands to light his cigar.

"Put that damn' thing out," the sheriff breathed softly, excitedly. "You want your face shot in?"

Matt shook the match out, saying apologetically: "Didn't think, I reckon. You really do expect this Big Bill, Sheriff?"

"You're damn' right I do!"

"Then you lead right on. Show me how to get to the street from here. I'll watch this side from the . . . from the front."

Matt's last three words had been spoken more loudly than the rest. For a moment ago a sound had shuttled along the alley, and, standing as he was now, he saw a shadow moving across toward the bank's rear wall from a shed across the way.

He breathed a vast sigh of relief—Case was in the passageway, unable to see. Now he quickly turned and made plenty of noise in stumbling after the lawman up the length of the narrow corridor. Big Bill was on his way into the bank. He could only hope that Bill would follow the rest of his instructions to the letter.

Case stopped at the head of the passageway, saying in a low voice: "Now, if I was you, I'd stand right here. You can see both ways along the street, and, if there's any trouble out back, I'll holler."

"Better make it good and loud."

"I will." The lawman stepped out onto the walk.

Matt watched him saunter along the front of the bank and try the doors. Then he went on.

By that time Matt already had one boot off and was pulling at the other. Then Case stepped out of sight into the passageway along the bank's far wall. Laying his boots aside and drawing one of his Colts, Matt turned and cat-footed quickly back along his corridor to the alley. When he turned into the alley, it was to hug the shadows close to the wall.

He ran the last few steps across to the foot of that far passageway, making no noise, and as a last precaution took off his hat and dropped it, coming to a crouch at the wall end. His head low to the ground, he looked around the corner.

He heard Case stumbling toward him close by. But it was so black down that narrow alleyway that he couldn't see so much as a shadow. There was barely time for him to come erect and lift the .45 before Clyde Case stepped out into the open.

Once he had his target, Matt swung his blow expertly. The barrel of the Colt caught the sheriff above the ear, denting in the side of his hat. Case sighed softly. His knees buckled. It was no trick at all for Matt to catch him as he fell, unconscious.

Matt laid the lawman down gently, wheeling immediately to walk over to the boarded-up section of the wall. He holstered the Colt as he pulled aside the loose board and whispered: "OK, Bill. Everything's set."

He had barely spoken before the big man edged sideways through the narrow opening that barely let him squeeze through. Bill carried a bulging gunny sack in each hand and one of these he quickly held out to Matt, saying brusquely: "Here, take it."

Matt took the sack and hefted it, asking: "How'd it go?"

Bill chuckled in a deep, excited voice. "Nothin' to it. Didn't even have to use the knife. Brother, we made a haul! Now how do I get out of here?"

"Just the way you came, Bill."

Matt was still speaking when Bill made a sudden move, his ham-like fist awkwardly pulling the Navy Colt from holster. As he leveled the weapon at Matt and backed away a step, he snarled: "Reach for the back of your neck, runt!"

Matt was careful to keep his hands well away from his sides as he dropped the sack and lifted them. As he locked his hands behind his neck, Bill said hoarsely: "I told you no one had ever double-crossed me!"

"No one's tryin' to double-cross you, Bill."

"Damn' right they ain't!" Bill said. He started backing away into the shadows. "You just stay set till I'm gone, runt! If you move a finger, I let daylight through you!"

Matt wasn't particularly alarmed. But he stayed as he was for better than a minute after Bill had edged out of sight into the blackness. At the end of that interval he thought he heard the slow hoof falls of a horse going away across the rocky hillside above the alley.

Yet he wasn't sure Bill had gone until he softly called: "You still there?"

There was no answer, and, letting out a gusty breath, he brought his hands down. He picked up the sack and reached into it. A slow smile came to his face as he brought out a handful of paper. Even in this faint light he could see that it was scrap paper.

When he had emptied the sack, he found that it contained nothing but more scrap paper, a bundle of blotters, several unused tablets, and two empty ink bottles. Something struck him as being very funny then and he laughed softly as he stuffed the worthless junk back into the sack.

He took one parting look at Sheriff Case before he moved back up to his own passageway. When he brushed against the rain barrel, he lifted the lid, dropped the sack into it, replaced the lid, and went on.

He pulled on his boots again, went to the street head of the passageway, and sat down. He was a man of patience and made himself comfortable as he settled there to wait.

Some ten minutes later a man with a shotgun cradled in the bend of his arm came sauntering along the far walk. By the time he was abreast, Matt had rolled up a smoke. He took some pains to see that the match flared openly as he lit it.

As though that had been a prearranged signal, the man over there left the walk and angled toward him. Halfway across, he called softly: "That you, Clyde?"

"Nope," Matt answered. "Clyde's out back."

It was one of the men who had gone with Mayor Williams. "Nothin' doin' so far as I can see," he told Matt as he joined him. "Think I'll go chew the fat with Clyde for a while."

"This is a lot of hogwash." Matt yawned. "No one's goin' to bust into this place. Wish I could get some sleep."

"Me, too. Let's see if I can talk Clyde into lettin' us call it off." The man walked away, taking the far passageway toward the bank's rear.

It came sooner than Matt had expected, in less than a minute, in fact. Suddenly a shout echoed up out of the alley. It was high-pitched, almost a scream. Matt grinned and, just to see what would happen, drew one of his Colts. He pointed it roofward along the passageway and thumbed three fast, deafening shots, bellowing: "Stop! Stop!"

Hardly had the sound of his shots died out before someone yelled stridently far up the street. A shotgun's boom rode over the town as Matt ran back toward the alley. He had nearly reached it when the man back there shouted: "Don't shoot! It's me . . . Red."

Matt, turning into the alley, called breathlessly: "Did you get him?"

"Who?"

"How would I know who?" Matt said acidly. "Who was it you yelled at? I saw him cross right here goin' down the alley."

"I didn't yell at no one. It's Clyde."

"So it was Clyde?" Matt asked, hearing others running toward them along the alley now.

"Hell, no, it wasn't Clyde! It was, I mean! He's here. Out cold!" Now at the sound of quick-pounding boots coming along the alley the speaker lifted his voice again, bawling: "Damn it, don't none of you shoot!"

Shortly one of the men who gathered about the sheriff lit a lantern and, as confused talk began, at least two men claimed to have seen a rider heading out of the alley. But they had seen this supposed rider going in opposite directions and Matt added to the confusion by giving his version of having shot at someone afoot.

Suddenly a man at the back fringe of the crowd bawled out: "God A'mighty, here's a loose board!"

"Where?"

"Where the hell you think? Here!"

The others forgot their unconscious sheriff then and crowded around the man who was reaching out to pull the loose board in the wall aside. As he did so, several groans escaped the others. Someone breathed in an awed whisper—"The safe!"—and pushed the first man out of the way to squeeze in through the opening. The rest, hit by a sudden panic, started shoving and crowding forward, trying to be the first to follow the leader.

The man with the lantern was the last one in, and, as the wavering light thinned the corners of the big room, he was the only one who found the voice to speak. "Cleaned!"

Big Bill had made a mess of things. Papers were strewn every which way in front of the safe's open door. Several empty metal boxes, their lids twisted off, lay in the litter. A rack of trays from the safe sat in a lopsided stack on the floor of the nearest teller's cage.

When no one spoke over quite an interval, Matt said: "We're wastin' time, gents. Let's throw our hulls on some nags and take a look around."

But the man nearest him slowly shook his head. "Wouldn't be no use, mister," he said. "Whoever did it was smart enough to head for the pass off north of here."

"Then let's get up there and head him off."

"Unh-uh! That's cattle country beyond. No sheep-man's used that pass for the last ten years and ever come back."

Once again a weighty silence settled over the eerily lit room. These men were speechless, dumb-founded, staring fixedly at the open safe. Shortly one of them breathed in a hushed voice: "Not one damn' dollar left! We're stone broke! You and me and all the rest! Even Caleb West!"

Only then did the full impact of their predicament seem to strike home to them. They looked at each other stupidly, disbelievingly.

It was in this moment that Matt quietly told them: "Don't get in such a lather, boys. When we find out how much is missin', maybe I can help."

V

Only one thing had gone amiss in all of Matt's calculations. The next morning after breakfast he ambled on along the street past the crowd gathered in front of the bank as far as the livery corral. The palomino was gone. *Well,* he thought, *I reckon Whitey and the money are both at the same place.* He really didn't feel very bad about it, nor was he very surprised.

Along about nine o'clock, as he sat on the hotel verandah, a man came over from the bank and stopped below him on the walk, saying respectfully: "Caleb West and the directors would like to see you across there, Mister North."

Matt said—"Sure."—and came down off the verandah to walk back with the man. The crowd in front of the bank, such a big one that it spilled off the walk into the street, opened silently before him and his companion, and on his way to the doors he heard a woman say in a loud whisper: "That's him. They say he's our only hope."

Inside, on the way to Caleb West's private office, Matt saw that no attempt had been made at cleaning up the litter alongside the safe.

There were eight men in the banker's office, which was clouded with cigar smoke. The four sitting at the long table at the room's center rose respectfully at Matt's entry and it was West himself who offered his chair, saying: "Here, sit at the head, Matt."

But Matt shook his head. "Always did think better on my feet, thanks." He pulled his coat open, thrust hands in pockets, and went to stand with his back to the window, asking abruptly: "What's on your minds?"

Caleb West cleared his throat. With a nervous glance at the others he began: "Well, Matt . . . Mister North, that is . . . we're sort of . . . well, I guess you'd say . . . "

"I guess your bank is about busted," Matt cut in. "Is that what you're tryin' to say, Caleb?"

The banker nodded glumly.

"And you want to know if I'm goin' to help you?" Matt asked.

"Well, we kinda hoped you'd . . . "

"Let's not beat about the bush," Matt interrupted again, rather sharply this time. "You've had some bad luck. If you close your doors, this range dries up and blows away. You need ready cash to stay in business. Correct?"

"You said a mouthful," Mayor Williams put in quietly.

"How much did you lose?"

"Eighty-seven thousand four hundred two dollars and sixty-nine cents," the banker stated.

Matt's soft whistle was absolutely genuine. "Now that's a wad of money, even for me," he drawled, frowning. He had never been particularly quick at figures and now, after a few seconds, asked: "How much would it take to keep you on your feet?"

Caleb West shrugged worriedly. "That's a matter of question, Matt."

Let's see, Matt was thinking, *Ives is asking thirty for the layout. Thirty from eighty-seven odd is . . . is around fifty some.* And he asked: "Could you limp along on fifty thousand?"

The gladness that replaced the worry on Caleb's face was really touching. "We could, Matt, we could. And every man, woman, and child in the valley would thank you from the bottoms of their hearts."

Matt was impressed but tried not to show it. In fact, he was frowning as he drawled: "I can swing that much without too much trouble." There was an excited mutter of voices at the table and now Mayor Williams and the others sat straighter, looking less like a pack of whipped dogs.

"But," Matt went on, "there's one big hitch. Maybe you remember me sayin' a couple times yesterday that I don't take to sheep."

They looked at each other nervously and with some alarm and Mayor Williams said: "Matt, it's somethin' you can get used to."

Matt shook his head. "Not me." He let those words lie by themselves over the following silence.

Shortly a man at the table's far end asked meekly: "Then it's no go?"

"If you stick to sheep," Matt told him. "Look, gents," he continued with a seemingly vast patience, "I just happened to stop here because this valley looked good. And because I was lookin' around for a few hundred or so sections of land to throw some beef onto."

"A few hundred?" Williams breathed in awe. "But there ain't that much for sale around here."

"There will be if I pull out and wait maybe a year," Matt reminded him. "Let this bank go broke and in a year I can buy land here at thirty cents on the dollar."

"You wouldn't do that, Matt," Caleb West said in a small voice.

"I damn' well would if it's either that or live around the stink of sheep."

When he had finished speaking, they looked at each other skeptically. It was finally Williams who had the nerve to speak up: "That's puttin' it to us straight, boys. I, for one, could live just as long if Jenny never cooked another of those mutton shoulder roasts." He shuddered convincingly. "And the air around here could be a bit sweeter."

"Cattle will pay a man almost as good as sheep," Caleb conceded.

Then one of the others banged his fist on the table, saying tartly: "I'm switchin' over! I was raised to hate sheep and here I been messin' with a wool crop the past ten years." He sighed audibly, feelingly. "It'll be a relief to ship them stinkin' critters and settle down to some clean, honest ranchin'."

There was more talk, a lot more, but by the time the courthouse clock was striking ten Matt was astride a livery horse and leaving the town behind him. Everything was settled. For a long-term loan of fifty thousand dollars, the directors guaranteed him that any outfit doing business with the bank would either change over to beef or be denied any financial help whatsoever. There were hardly any brands in the valley that could get along without bank money at some time or another.

So he was whistling as he rode along. He was on his way, so he told them, over the pass to the railroad to have the money sent in by express. He had assumed a distant air when they became curious as to his background. Thinking back on that, he could smile now. Just for the fun of it, he went through his pockets to see exactly what he was worth. The total came to $4.60 and in this moment he reflected somewhat bleakly that he would have to stay away from poker layouts, one having rid him of a year's savings two nights before he started over the pass to meet Jesúsita.

Sita! He'd had too much on his mind to spare her many thoughts, but now she became the core about which much of his thinking revolved. He was still trying to picture the brightness of her eyes, her slenderness and grace, and wondering how much room there was in her heart for such a man as he when he brought the *cantina* in sight two hours later.

He was swinging from the saddle at the rail by the *portal* when the doors swung open to frame a vision of radiant loveliness for him. Her black, wavy hair shone like ebony and fell loosely about her shoulders. Those gently rounded shoulders were half revealed by a white embroidered blouse of some filmy material that barely clung to them. About her small waist ran a belt of broad silver *conchas* and below that a long black silk skirt nearly swept the dust as she ran out, white petticoats showing, to cry:

"Matt. Oh my poor Matt! I all the time theenk you keeled!"

He couldn't help but put his arms about her as she threw herself against him. And then, unashamedly, she took his face in her hands and pulled it down to smother it with kisses. She kissed his cheeks, chin, eyes, and then his mouth. Finally, to get a breath, she drew away, and her flashing dark eyes laughed up at him. Then all at once her look turned grave, alarmed. "Matt, you hide queek! Beeg Beel, he's around somewheres. He tell me he keel you, pool your arms off, and heet you in the face weeth them. All in the fight over me. So, last night I cry, and thees morning I still cry and Beel, he say I am his now because he won me from you. I heet him again but he only laugh. And then I find he gives Papa the monee, lots of *dinero*. So Papa, he tell me we go across to the town weeth the railroad and be married. And now Beel somew'ere out back heetching the team for the treep. Oh, Matt, now you save me from Beel!"

"That I'll do," Matt drawled.

He took her by the shoulders, the excitement strong in him as he said: "But first, we got to get something settled, *muchacha*. Down in the valley there's a ranch. It's got a big house of 'dobe shaped like the letter H. There's cottonwoods and willows all 'round and a crick runnin' right past the porch. And off behind there are hills covered with pines and down below there's a meadow with a big ponderosa standin' square in the middle of it all by itself and . . . "

"The Anvil, the Reevers' place," Jesúsita put in, nodding quickly. "Papa, he work there for old Matt

Reevers before the sheepmans, she come. He was the wan fine *vaquero*. And Papa, he steel tell how he teach the leetle Reevers to ride, the leetle boy."

Matt's look became a wondering one and he asked: "Papa couldn't be Miguel, could he?"

"Miguel, sure. He's Papa. Why? You know heem?"

"No. I . . . that is, someone down below mentioned him to me." Then, to cover his confusion, he shook her gently by the shoulders, saying: "Sita, I've just bought the . . . "

His words broke off a fraction of a second as he noticed the *cantina*'s swing doors slowly inching apart. He waited to be sure that they didn't open any farther before going on in a louder voice: "I've just bought the Anvil. How would Papa and your brother like to come there to live? Papa could look after the horse string all on his own. Your brother would maybe run the kitchen for the crew. How does that sound?"

"Everisto, he my cosin." There was a warmth and a tenderness in her eyes as she looked up at him, softly asking: "And me, Matt?"

Matt shrugged, finding it hard to speak. "That's up to you, Sita. I'm nothin' but a top hand that's been pretty fiddle-footed and never saved a nickel. Maybe I'd make you a poor husband."

"Oh, Matt!"

Again she threw her arms around him and kissed his face, and now Matt noticed the doors come open violently. Inside, in the deep shadow, he saw a high shape and his frame went rigid.

But then the doors swung slowly shut once more and he breathed a sigh of relief and gave his attention to the immediate problem.

Jesúsita was saying excitedly: "We go now, thees afternoon! I shot thees place, lock it and leave it forever. Wait, I tell Papa and Everisto." She whirled and ran to the door.

From out back came the soft squeal of door hinges. Matt, putting his own meaning to the sound, said loudly although he was talking to himself: "Big Bill's wanted on about ten counts. He'll hang if he ever shows his face in this country again."

He went silent a moment and now heard the slow, measured hoof thuds of a horse he assumed was walking toward him along the *cantina*'s far wall. As he moved in toward the adobe wall that enclosed the *portal*, he went on speaking in that same loud voice: "There's a big reward out on him, if you get him, and . . . "

The palomino, Big Bill in the saddle, suddenly lunged into the open from around the building's far front corner. The Navy Colt was in Bill's hand. It swung down and into line with Matt as Matt forgot his dignity and dove sprawling behind the wall.

A sudden, deafening explosion marked the instant adobe plaster sprayed from the top of the wall. Over the fast drumming of the palomino's hoofs rose Big Bill's strident shout: "Come on out and fight, runt!"

Matt's impulse was to reach for one of his .45s. Instead, he smiled. Then, taking off his hat, he crawled to the wall's edge and looked out to the road.

The palomino was running fast, already out of sure range for a Colt. Yet Bill, facing about in the saddle, threw two more shots at the wall and Matt had to duck back again to keep from getting bullet-splashed dirt in his eyes.

Several seconds later Matt came erect and stepped

out into the open. The palomino's swift-reaching run was something to delight the eye and for a moment he watched in admiration. But Big Bill was headed toward the pass as fast as he could ride and this realization suddenly sobered Matt. He breathed: "The poor fool never learns."

Then, putting fingers between his lips, he gave a piercing whistle, so loud that the echo of it racketed back from the near piney slope.

He was watching the palomino's stride break as Jesúsita ran out through the doors crying: "Matt! Who is the shots?"

"Watch!" was all Matt said. She looked up the trail in time to see the horse slide to a sudden stop, then rear sharply, viciously. But this time Big Bill wasn't unseated as he had been here in front of the *cantina* yesterday. He dug in his spurs, grabbed the horn, and commenced sawing at the reins.

Matt's look turned worried. He lifted his hand again, whistled once more.

This had its immediate effect. The palomino came down on all four hoofs. Then suddenly his forelegs buckled, his head went down, and it was all Big Bill could do to take his boot from stirrup and jump for his life as the horse threatened to roll onto him.

Matt would have lost a horse then if the palomino hadn't been fast getting onto his feet again and going away. For Bill, lying there in the dust, had to roll over to pull his Colt.

Bill's first shot struck between the horse's flying hoofs. His second was wild because Matt had quickly drawn one of the .45s and thrown a shot at him. A geyser of dust spurted up two feet out from Bill's head. Then, as Matt fired again, the big man hauled himself to his feet and started running in panic. Never had Big Bill made such tracks. He went out the trail almost as fast as the palomino was running in along it. Just for the fun of it, Matt deliberately took another shot and still another.

"Keel heem!" Jesúsita cried, her eyes flashing hate at the big man. "Keel heem dead, Matt!"

Possibly, had his next shot been lucky, Matt could have winged Big Bill. But he was telling himself: *He's scared, really scared, and he'll never be back.* So he threw the bullet a pace or two ahead of Bill and to one side. Now he burst out laughing as Bill dodged aside, stumbled, rolled in the dust, and picked himself up again.

Jesúsita was laughing, too, as Bill rounded a far bend and disappeared behind the pines. "Beel, he have the sore feet tonight," she said, turning to Matt.

But he wasn't looking her way. The palomino, chest heaving, was standing beside him now and with one hand he was stroking the animal's neck while the other fumbled at the thongs of the nearest pouch on the saddle's cantle. He got the pouch open finally and looked inside. Jesúsita, not understanding his relieved smile just then, asked: "What ees it, Matt?"

"Nothin'," he drawled, tying the pouch's thong once more. "Nothin' at all. Just something I loaned Bill last night. For a minute there I thought he forgot to give it back."

He faced her again, grinning broadly.

"Now let's get a move on, Sita. I'd like to have a look at that layout before dark."

Posse of Outlawed Men

This was the fifth Western story Jon Glidden sold. It was submitted to the Popular Publications' Western pulp magazines in July, 1937 and was purchased by editor Mike Tilden on January 11, 1937. The author was paid $90. The story appeared in *Big-Book Western* (3–4/37).

I

An air of tense expectancy ran through the crowd that milled in the dusty street before the courthouse of Singletree. It was the appearance of a black-garbed figure in the doorway of the building that abruptly quieted the undertone of conversation. All eyes turned upward to watch the man as he came to the head of the steps, flanked by four sober-faced, gun-belted men. His glance shuttled briefly over the throng below before he sauntered down, seemingly unaware of the presence of these watchers.

He made an impressive figure even though he was shorter than the average in this country of tall men. In his swaggering walk, the outthrust chin, and in the gray eyes that were hard as polished granite there was a suggestion of rugged strength that made up for his lack of height.

At the foot of the steps the crowd gave way and the little knot of men passed through and across the street. Covertly hostile glances followed them, but it was obvious that the man and his bodyguard commanded a belligerent respect.

Ahead of him, one of his guards turned in from the awninged walk to shoulder through the slatted doors of a saloon. Inside, the gunman stopped in mid-stride, his right hand falling smoothly to the butt of the Colt, tied low on his thigh.

"Easy, Ace!" ordered the man in black to his guard as he pushed into the saloon a moment later, and at the command the guard's poised hand dropped away from the gun butt.

The man in black squinted a little, searching through the half light of the room until he saw the lone man who stood quietly regarding him from the center of the bar to his left. There were others there, too, but they stood across the room and he ignored them.

"I thought I told you to leave Singletree, Montana," he said.

The shadow of a smile played across the angular features of the man called Montana. His brown eyes glinted with some inner amusement, and then the look hardened as his face went expressionless.

"I don't scare easy, Frazer," he answered levelly, shifting his backthrust elbows a little on the bar top. "Thought I'd hang around and see you finish the framin'!"

Frazer blushed at the words. "You're makin' big talk!" he rasped, spacing his words carefully to hide his annoyance. The hard lines of his thin-lipped face made him ugly as he edged forward a little to give the others behind him room to enter.

"Nothin' I'm sayin' that I won't back up," Montana drawled tauntingly. "Any time."

Effortlessly Montana pushed himself erect from his slouch against the bar. His tall, flat-hipped frame was deceptively relaxed as he stood there calmly surveying the five men at the door. From the crown of his soiled Stetson to the toes of his soft, high-heeled boots he was quietly alert.

Behind Frazer there was the hint of a stealthy movement. At this instant Montana lunged sideways, his hand sweeping downward and rising in a blasting stab of flame. The man behind Frazer spun about, crashing into the wall, and a choked cry broke from his twisted lips. The Colt he had been swinging upward pounded solidly to the floor and a splotch of crimson spread across his right shoulder. The others stood, unmoving, tense, and watchful, ignoring the wounded man's muttered oaths.

The smoke curled upward from the blue snout of the Colt as Montana straightened and once more took his position at the bar. He flicked the .45 back into his worn holster. "Anybody else want more o' that medicine?" he asked in quiet defiance.

For seconds the air was heavy with impending action; the silence was like that interval between a lightning flash and the ensuing thunder. It was a silence that branded these five men at the door as nerveless, standing as they were before the deadly gun-swift hand of this drawling cowpuncher.

A shout from the outside broke the tension. Through the doors slammed a tall, shad-bellied oldster wearing a sheriff's badge. He stood glaring about, his black-browed gaze fixed for an instant on the wounded man who still leaned against the wall, then abruptly he singled out Montana.

"What the hell's this?" he boomed, standing with feet spread a little, and pushing his hat onto the back of his hairless head.

"You missed it, lawman!" Montana told him. "This sidewinder. . . ."

"Arrest him, Canby!" Frazer cut in.

The sheriff looked first at Montana, then at Frazer, and finally back again at Montana. "You're under arrest, Pierce," the lawman echoed in compliance with the order of the man in black. "I'm damned if I'll let any gunslinger raise this kind of hell in Singletree."

Montana calmly surveyed the sheriff. Finally he spoke, stopping Canby's move to come forward.

"Frazer, why don't you get the rest o' your outfit? Send out for Judge Solom, some more o' your Bar Z hairpins, and your open-range homesteaders that sat the jury today. So they convicted Clem Walker. You framed him and made it stick. Maybe with enough men backin' you, you'd make this new stunt of yours stick. As it is, you're plumb harmless."

"Pierce, you're under arrest," Canby repeated, but now his tone had none of the certainty it had had a moment before. "Hand over your hardware."

Montana's wary glance shuttled over to Frazer and his men, finally coming back to Canby. "And here we have a lawman," he sneered in mocking derision. "Canby, if you come one step closer, I'll blow you hell to breakfast."

He leaned forward a little, and again there was that flip of his hand that brought his Colt hip-high, covering the men in front of him before they could move. He sidled away from the bar, circling toward an open window that let out onto the street, moving with a cat-like ease. Frazer and his men pivoted as he moved, following him with their eyes.

When he stood at the window, he said: "There's six o' you standin' there. Why doesn't someone make a play? Canby, next time you try to make an arrest have someone along who'll back your play."

Montana stepped through the window. Frazer let out an oath and turned toward the doors, pushing his men ahead of him. Canby crowded behind, drawing his two .45s. Outside, the Bar Z gunmen came to an abrupt halt. Montana had waited beside the window and now held the steady muzzles of his Colts lined at the group.

"You gents stay set," he told them. "I'm headed up this alley. The first ranny who follows me gets cut to doll rags."

Lazily he stepped backward, a tight smile of reckless challenge on his lips. Abruptly he was gone.

Frazer cursed his men, but not one of them attempted to follow. Canby finally pushed through and started for the alley, broke into a run when the pounding of hoofs echoed between the buildings. When he turned into the alley, it was empty.

Across the street, on the courthouse steps, stood two people who had witnessed what had gone on in the street. One of them was a girl of perhaps twenty whose quizzical, hazel-eyed glance traveled up to the end of the street where a rider suddenly appeared from between two adobe houses.

"There he goes, Jim!" she said, speaking to the man who stood beside her. "What does it mean?"

"Mean?" he echoed, his wrinkled face lined with a frown. "Nothin'."

"That was Montana Pierce, Jim."

"Uhn-huh. He quit workin' for Frazer the day your dad was arrested."

"He had a gun on Canby and Frazer," she said, puzzlement written on her ivory-tinted face. "That's queer."

"What's queer about it?" Jim asked. "Those trigger-wizards are always havin' scrapes. Montana's just another Bar Z polecat, Miss Betty."

She was silent a moment, looking across the street to where the crowd milled about the saloon entrance. "Perhaps he's broken with Frazer after this. Any decent man would."

Jim snorted. "Miss Betty, you're forgettin' that it was men like Montana and Frazer that put your dad behind the bars."

Betty shook her head. "But he's different," she insisted. "I don't believe Montana took any part in what they did to Dad."

"Don't let him fool you," Jim told her. "He's just another no-account gunslingin' saddle bum or he wouldn't have hired out to Frazer in the first place. He probably helped Frazer plant that stolen herd in our pasture."

"You don't know it was Frazer!" she flared. "How can you be so sure?"

"Common sense," Jim reasoned. "Who else would want to get Clem Walker out of the way? Who's hoggin' the range and drivin' the little fellow off? It couldn't be anyone but Frazer. He's after the Circle W water, and he'll get it one way or another. And just because we're strangers here . . . because only three years on this range still makes us strangers . . . these gutless people are goin' to stand by and let him do it."

"There must be enough decent people around to stop a thing like that."

"There aren't!" Jim asserted explosively. "The trial today showed they're lily-livered when it comes to buckin' the Bar Z. It was one of Frazer's hands who found the rustled stock in our pasture and reported it to Canby. It was a parcel of Frazer's open-range homesteaders on the jury today that found your dad guilty. The idea of Clem Walker bein' convicted on a rustlin' charge may seem addle-headed to us because we know him, but he's still a stranger in this country. Frazer framed Clem Walker, had him tried, and is makin' it stick."

"Let's ride, Jim," Betty sighed. "I've got to get out of here."

II

They went out into the street, followed by the curious glances of those about them, got their horses at the livery stable, and headed out of town. They rode out across the bench-like grasslands that stretched away toward the low, hazy foothills. It was mid-afternoon and the sun's glow made the shimmering distance deceptive so that the jagged peaks of the Antelopes seemed far off and floating in an ocean of blue fog.

"What's next?" Betty Walker finally asked in a small voice. "Will you be lookin' for another job, Jim?"

Jim jerked a sideward glance at her and half turned in the saddle. "Do you think I'm leavin' after sidin' Clem for the last ten years?" His glance softened as he took in Betty's drooping figure. "We'll get through this some way. Don't you fret about that."

Betty was silent, half-heartedly glad that things were finally settled. The last few days had been slow torture for her. Clem Walker's arrest had come without warning, and the three days since he entered jail had been spent in a frantic, useless search for evidence that would prove his innocence. Now it was over and to be in the saddle once again and riding through the stillness of this vast open range was a relief, yet it left her feeling alone and weary. Jim, for the first time, now saw the worry that Betty had so well concealed for the past few days written plainly on her fine-featured face.

"We'll go 'long without Clem for a spell, Miss Betty," Jim said. "Give me a little time and I'll hunt down the coyotes that planted that wet beef on us. It won't be long before your dad's back again."

The shadow of some inner thought took the light out of her eyes. "Jim, I haven't told you, but we're in bad shape." Her face was averted and he could not read the expression on it.

"Bad shape?" he echoed. "Oh, well, we'll make out."

"Not if the herds keep falling off," she insisted. "We aren't going to have much of a count this roundup."

"We'll see they don't fall off any more."

"How can we? We haven't the money to hire the men it would take to guard them. No, Jim! Unless we can get Dad back to run things, we'll be cleaned out before another year rolls around."

Suddenly realizing that she was right, Jim made no attempt to deny the fact. This thing had been uppermost in his mind even before the calamity of Clem's arrest struck them. The fire went out of him and he slouched in the saddle, his spare figure drooping with an utter weariness.

"Somethin' may happen to help," he said lamely and without conviction.

A heavy silence hung over them for the rest of their ten-mile ride. Long before the weathered frame buildings of the Circle W rose up out of the distance, the sky had banked with black thunder clouds, seeming to suit their mood. The breeze that had been gently stirring across the distances gave way to a sultry stillness and the heat became oppressive. The sun, red for the past hour, finally lost itself in a haze that rose up out of the far-off mountain valleys.

"The arroyos'll be runnin' water before sundown," Jim said. Betty made no answer, and he could not be sure that she had heard.

The storm began in a low muttering of distant thunder, shortly before the too-early darkness blanketed down over the plain. For an hour a hushed stillness deadened all the evening sounds, then the rain started, slowly at first, coming down in huge splashing drops until it gathered in volume to a pelting downpour.

Under the protection of the wide porch that ran across the face of the bunkhouse, Jim and two others sat in the darkness, watching the storm. The two, along with two more riders who were now at a line camp in the hills, completed the Circle W crew that had formerly numbered a dozen riders.

Clem Walker had let his men go one by one as the spread drifted toward certain financial ruin. Rustling had taken a heavy toll on the herds, and Walker, powerless to keep them guarded in the face of a constant danger, had seen the Circle W sapped of all its strength. Now, no longer drawing pay, these four were staying on out of sheer loyalty to a man they had learned to respect deeply.

The three of them were wordless, watching in complete silence the ferocity of the storm. Sharp, rolling bursts of thunder punctuated the lightning flashes that showed the drenched landscape in the distance. The steady drone of the downpour filled in the intervals between the lightning crashes.

The road that led away from the yard was running water that had already cut deep gashes in the loose, rutted soil. In the brief glimpses they had of it, they could follow the course of the torrent until it dropped into an arroyo at the foot of the slope.

In one of those split-second flashes they saw a rider outlined against the grayness beyond, coming up the road, his horse at a walk. Jim got up out of his chair, waited impatiently for the few seconds until there was another lightning flash and he could see the man again.

"Get your irons," he ordered finally, and the other two faded through the inky shadow of the doorway. When they returned, he told them: "He's headin' for the house. Rick, you go over and get in the back way. Don't show a light until you savvy what this is all about. Al and I will go out front and meet him. It may not mean trouble, but there's a lot of two-legged coyotes loose on this range. We can't take chances with Miss Betty here."

None of them took the time to get their ponchos, but, dressed as they were, they ran out into the storm and across to the house. Jim and Al had waited less than ten seconds when there was a call from out front.

"Hello!"

"Hello, yourself!" Jim answered. "Who is it?"

"Montana Pierce!"

Montana sat hunched over in the saddle, his face shielded against the driving rain by the rim of his Stetson, waiting for the voice he had recognized as Jim Early's to reply. He was about to shout out his name again, thinking he had not been heard, when Jim finally spoke gruffly out of the blackness of the porch: "Light and come on in!"

Montana swung stiffly to the ground, unbuckled his poncho, and threw it over his saddle. "Hell of a night," he said as he stepped in under the wide porch roof.

"What'll you have?" Jim asked in unwelcome abruptness.

"I rode out to see Miss Walker."

"Maybe she don't want to see you," came Jim's blunt statement. "Frazer's gunmen aren't welcome here."

A rectangle of light all at once flooded out onto the porch as the house door swung open. Framed in the light was Betty Walker's straight, delicately rounded figure.

"Jim," she said, "any man's welcome in this storm. Come in, Montana!"

Montana followed her into the house, feeling a little awkward in her presence, wondering if he should have chosen this way of helping her. His eyes followed her every move, tasting the peculiar thrill it gave him to be this close to her. Betty Walker affected him that way; strangely, too, for Montana was unwilling to admit to himself, even yet, that any woman could interest him. She seemed more real than other girls he had known, for there was no pretense about her. When she spoke, her mellow tones carried a conviction that was heightened by the direction of the look in her hazel eyes.

Montana had never thought of her as being beautiful, yet instinctively he knew that she was. Her perfectly formed features were set in a strong though delicately feminine face that was expressive of her every mood. There was a poise about her that showed strength and character. Even now, knowing that she must be wearied to the core over the events of the day, he saw that her boyishly square shoulders were back, her carriage erect, and her chin set in clear indication she was not beaten.

"You've got a lot of explainin' to do, Montana," Jim spoke up. "Let's have it."

"I heard you needed a man out here," Montana said, speaking to Betty. "I came out for the job."

"We told no one we needed a man," she answered him, a puzzled frown wrinkling her high forehead.

"I reckon you didn't," he admitted. "But you'll be needin' help now with your dad gone."

"We're lookin' out for ourselves," Jim's voice boomed. "We don't have any use for gunslingers!"

"I can rope and ride better'n any man on this spread," Montana told Jim levelly.

"Get this, Montana . . . ," Jim began.

"But it's true, Jim," Betty cut in. "We need more . . . any men who'll take our starvation wages."

Jim turned somber eyes on her. "I've worked for Clem Walker the best part of my life and we've never had to hire gun jacks to keep our own. It's too late to start now. If you want to take Pierce on, you don't want me." His glance swung around to rake Montana.

"I reckon I'll go," Montana answered. "I only wanted to help."

Jim said: "If you want to help, then ride out of here."

Montana smiled meagerly, shrugged, and turned away. He might have expected this. Deep within him he knew that Jim belonged here—that it was no choice Betty could make. If the Circle W was to go down, it would go down Clem Walker's way— string-straight and fine.

He crossed the porch and walked out through the driving downpour to where his thick-shouldered chestnut gelding stood with down-hanging head. His movements were mechanical as he threw on his poncho, climbed into the saddle, and rode away. This way, then, was closed.

Once before he had seen men make their own law, as Frazer was doing. That time five forked men had driven him out of the Coconino Sink—had driven him to killing two of them. It was a hard lesson, but he had learned it. If it had worked once for them, it would work again, for him.

So, two days afterward, he faced five more men. But this time the five men were listening to him. It was in a shack far up Bitter Creek Cañon. He had chosen well. Each man hated Frazer, had been robbed, broken, beaten by him.

Of them all, Peewee Steele was the biggest and the most stubborn. His thoughtful face and his unhurried manner would be indicative of the thoughts of the rest. The time it took him to come to a decision would give Gabe Halpin time to cool off, Rand Avery time to recall the gun-whipping Ace Doolin had given him, and Ben Tilton time to let his old man's grudge freshen. Juan Mercado needed no urging; for two years he had been waiting for the chance to revenge Frazer's desertion of his sister.

His face unsmiling, his voice level, he had told them of his plan. He was completing his instructions to Peewee: "... So you see, you'll risk your neck, Peewee, but if it fails, you'll ride out of the country with the rest of us ... ride light, hard, hell for leather."

Gabe Halpin's long frame seemed to couple together as he lunged from the table, faced Peewee, and said softly: "This don't take thinkin' out, Peewee!"

Juan Mercado said: "Me, I'm theenk Frazer look more better weeth knife in his neck!"

"Some rannies would rather die that way than lose land," Ben Tilton said. "Frazer's one of 'em."

Rand Avery said, stroking a scar on his cheek: "We're only six but what the hell! I chance it."

"The two Wheeler boys are in it. I came from their layout this afternoon," Montana said. He had been saving this as a driving wedge.

Now they tangled. Ben Tilton was dubious, impervious to Gabe Halpin's scorn. Mercado had a different plan. Avery was quiet, watching Peewee. Finally Montana said: "How about it, Peewee?"

Peewee looked carefully at his fingernails and said slowly, softly: "Let's try it your way, Montana. If anything'll ever work, it will."

Montana's glance shuttled over these men. He said: "Do you all want it my way?"

When they nodded, his face relaxed for the first time. "Wheeler's spread is closest to the railroad. We can push 'em from Gabe's Rockin' H ..."

"Not mine any more," Gabe cut in bitterly. "Not since Frazer burned me out!"

Montana corrected himself. "We can push 'em from what used to be Gabe's place, over the *malpais*"—he allowed himself a down-bearing smile—"you rustlers!"

III

Shortly before daybreak Montana sat hunkered down, his back against a jack pine, scanning carefully a pasture that was bordered by the stand of timber in which he was hiding. In the ghostly light of the moon he could pick out the darker shadows that he knew were cattle. Here was the Bar Z pasture where Henry Crossan rode herd, and, if he was not mistaken, it was Henry Crossan who was slowly circling the herd and heading toward him.

It seemed an eternity before the rider came close enough for Montana to recognize him, yet when he saw the black and white checked shirt, he knew that he had found his man. He hailed him softly, and, as the sound of his voice drifted out across the still air, Crossan shifted suddenly in the saddle and his hand dipped to draw the carbine from the scabbard on the far side of his horse. He did not move for several seconds, but then advanced slowly toward Montana, his Winchester ready in the crook of his arm.

"What do you want?" he growled when he was still twenty yards away.

"Howdy, Henry!"

Crossan gave a visible start. "Well, I'll . . . !" The rest of his words were lost as he spurred forward and drew rein a short distance away. "Come out and show yourself!"

Montana came out into the light. "Did you think I'd skipped the country?" he asked.

"Hell, no," Henry replied. "Not you."

"Henry, we're out to cut in on Frazer's play," Montana told him, coming abruptly to the purpose of his visit. "Peewee, Gabe Halpin, the Wheeler boys, and a few others. Want to come in on it?"

In the strong light of the moon, Montana caught Henry's startled look, saw the broad grin that spread across his lean face. "Do I want in on it?" he exclaimed. "Am I loco? Sure, I'm in!"

Montana was silent a moment, then said: "I've been figurin', Henry. You're usin' the Bar Z as a hide-out from somethin' or other, or you wouldn't stay two minutes, ridin' herd for a sidewinder like Frazer."

Crossan gave him a long look before he replied. "Seems like more'n one of Frazer's hairpins is on the dodge. I don't deny it."

"Doesn't mean a thing to me." Montana shrugged. "Only I wanted to get it straight. I've heard you speak your mind once or twice about Frazer. I figure you're achin' to see him pay for a few of the things he's done. Well, so are the rest of us."

"Montana, if there's anything I can do to help you put that polecat at the end of a rope, I'm with you. When do we ride?"

Montana quickly ran over in his mind the things he knew about Crossan—his straightforwardness, his sincere loathing of Frazer's methods, and lastly that unspoken friendship that he had for the man. If he was any judge at all, Crossan would fit in with his plans.

"You're good to me right where you are," Montana said to him. "There's enough in our bunch to handle things on the outside. If you'll stay at the Bar Z and work from the inside, you'll be doin' the most good."

"What do I do?"

"Nothin' yet. In a day or so I'll be back. You'll be here?"

"I reckon," Henry replied. "I've been here three weeks now, and Frazer ain't goin' to take the guards off his critters."

They talked a few minutes more, and then Montana left, satisfied that Henry fitted in with the plans. An hour later he was four miles back in the hills where he made a fireless camp. As he lay in the blankets, looking up at the winking stars, he felt a strange elation. In planning all this he had not realized how willingly others would join him. Finally he closed his eyes, anxious that sleep should bring closer his meeting with Peewee and the rest.

A rope snaked down from above to coil half its length on a rocky ledge sixty feet above the cañon floor. As it etched its thin line against the star-sprinkled void of the sky, six dark silent figures came down it hand over hand to stand on the ledge.

Montana waited until Gabe stood beside him. "Which way?" he asked.

In answer Gabe moved off to his right, and they started down through the tumbled mass of rock and stunted piñon. Once Montana cautioned Gabe about going too fast, as Peewee loosed a small rock from above. Luckily it did not roll far, but from there on they proceeded with more caution.

Below, Montana could see the outlines of the three buildings, one larger than the others. This larger building was in the center of a barren plot of ground. Forty feet behind it, almost directly underneath their path, was a fringe of tall cedars. Darkness hid the cattle that Montana knew were grazing in the pasture that ran down the center of the wide cañon.

When they were in the trees just below, behind the house, Montana sent Juan off first, giving him a five-minute start before the others melted into the shadows after him. He stood with Gabe a moment, watching Peewee's bulk disappear through the trees. Then he stepped out, walked silently across the open stretch of ground to the rear of the main building. Quickly he crawled beneath an open window along the side wall and drew up at the front corner.

It took him ten long seconds to creep into the shadows of the unfloored porch, Gabe following closely behind. They waited a moment beside the open door, and then Montana abruptly stepped inside, drawing his Colt.

The silence of his entrance was unbroken for long moments. Then Gabe stepped in after him and there was an ominous creaking of a loose board. The low snoring of a man in a bunk at the right continued

GET 4 FREE BOOKS!

You can have the best Westerns delivered to your door for less than what you'd pay in a bookstore or online. Sign up for one of our book clubs today, and we'll send you **4 FREE* BOOKS**, worth $23.96, just for trying it out...**with no obligation to buy, ever!**

Authors include classic writers such as
LOUIS L'AMOUR, MAX BRAND, ZANE GREY
and more; PLUS new authors such as
COTTON SMITH, TIM CHAMPLIN, JOHNNY D. BOGGS
and others.

As a book club member you also receive the following special benefits:
- **30% OFF** all orders through our website & telecenter!
- **Exclusive access to special discounts!**
- **Convenient home delivery and 10 days to return any books you don't want to keep.**

There is no minimum number of books to buy,
and you may cancel membership at any time.
See back to sign up!

*Please include $2.00 for shipping and handling.

YES! ☐

Sign me up for the Leisure Western Book Club
and send my FOUR FREE BOOKS! If I choose to stay
in the club, I will pay only $14.00* each month,
a savings of $9.96!

NAME: _____

ADDRESS: _____

_____

TELEPHONE: _____

E-MAIL: _____

☐ **I WANT TO PAY BY CREDIT CARD.**

☐ **VISA**   ☐ **MasterCard.**   ☐ **DISCOVER**

ACCOUNT #: _____

EXPIRATION DATE: _____

SIGNATURE: _____

Send this card along with $2.00 shipping & handling to:

**Leisure Western Book Club
1 Mechanic Street
Norwalk, CT 06850-3431**

Or fax (must include credit card information!) to: 610.995.9274.
You can also sign up online at www.dorchesterpub.com.

*Plus $2.00 for shipping. Offer open to residents of the U.S. and Canada only.
Canadian residents please call 1.800.481.9191 for pricing information.
If under 18, a parent or guardian must sign. Terms, prices and conditions subject to change. Subscription subject
to acceptance. Dorchester Publishing reserves the right to reject any order or cancel any subscription.

JOIN NOW!

unbroken, but at once Montana heard a stealthy movement across the room.

"Who the hell's that?" came a voice the next instant. There was a short, tense silence. Then: "Wake up, boys! There's someone in here!"

Montana waited, heard the others stir. Across the room he heard a man climb from his bunk and move stealthily along the far wall.

Crash!

A thundering shot unexpectedly blasted the silence. Montana instinctively swung his Colt around, thumbed a shot at the floor in the direction of the gun flash.

"Throw down your cutters!" he called out sharply. "We've got the place surrounded!"

"Like hell!" came an angry snarl, punctuated with the crashing roar of a .45 that momentarily lighted the room with its purple flame stab. Gabe's Colt tore loose in an instantaneous answer. It was followed by a choked groan, and after a moment the dull thud of a body falling.

"Someone light the lamp!" came another voice. "Bill's hurt bad."

"Don't be a damn fool!" barked another. "There's two of 'em waitin' to cut down on us."

Montana groped about him, found Gabe, and pulled him by the sleeve along the wall and into a corner. Some instinct must have prompted him to change his position, for the next instant three .45s launched out a staccato blast from the other end of the room. The beating inferno of those shots had not yet died down when there came a crash as a table overturned, and the man opposite rushed to the spot where Gabe and Montana had been. Montana saw one of the figures framed in the paler light of the doorway. He swung the Colt around, felt it buck in his hand, then threw himself to the floor. As two .45s cut loose at the spot where he had stood, he saw the figure in the doorway stumble backwards and fall out onto the porch.

From outside came the muffled sound of two closely spaced shots. There was a momentary silence before three more shots thudded out. In the room no one moved. Montana waited.

"Let's cut loose of this place," came a loud whisper. "There's more outside."

Without stopping to answer, three figures plunged through the doorway. Montana and Gabe thumbed their .45s, spattering the floor near the door with their slugs, aiming low. The three gained the porch, only to be brought up short as Ben Tilton's voice boomed out of the darkness: "Stand where you are, gents!"

Montana was on his feet, and in two strides was standing at the door. "Reach!" he drawled quietly. "You're through."

In the dim light he saw the three hesitate one brief instant. He fired once, could see where the bullet kicked up the dust at their feet. At that, they dropped their six-guns, slowly raised their hands.

Montana and Gabe picked up their guns. Searching the men, Montana found two knives and a small, wicked-looking Derringer. As he stepped away and called to Ben, Peewee and Rand Avery rounded the back corner of the building, prodding before them two other prisoners.

"There's one ranny out there who won't ever straddle his hull again," Peewee announced.

"Ben, you and Gabe hightail down and help Juan with that guard," Montana said quickly. "If he's had any trouble. . . ."

"No one 'ave trouble, Montana!" came a voice close at hand. Juan came up out of the shadow. "The *hombre* up there keeck up wan beeg fuss. It was hees last."

"Take a look over here!" Peewee called out now, from around the corner of the building. Montana walked over, saw him bending over a prone figure on the ground. "Look what was tryin' to crawl away."

Montana looked more closely, and even in the dim light recognized the thin, hawk-like features of Peewee's captive.

"Howdy, Ace," Montana said levelly, trying to keep the surprise out of his face. "So you're runnin' this end of Frazer's business?"

"Pierce, your carcass won't be worth a spick *peso* when Frazer hears about this."

"Ace, you were along the other day in Singletree when I told Frazer I couldn't be scared out. I haven't changed my mind." He paused, but Ace made no answer, so he went on: "Peewee, look Ace over and patch him up. He's leadin' his gunmen home."

In ten minutes, five Bar Z horses stood with their riders lashed face down across their saddles, hands and feet laced together under the horses' bellies. Ace Doolin, the Bar Z ramrod, was astride his saddle with his feet bound tightly to the cinch.

Montana took Ben aside. "Take 'em as far as the

alfalfa this side of the breaks. Turn 'em loose and hightail over to Wheeler's. We'll meet you there sometime tomorrow."

"Montana!" came Ace's voice. "Loosen this damned rope! That spick's got me tied tighter 'n fence wire."

"I reckon you'll make it home all right, Ace," Montana answered. "Tell Frazer we went easy on you rannies tonight. Next time, it'll be different."

"You figure Frazer 'll let this go by without huntin' you down?" Ace snarled.

"I've quit tryin' to figure him," Montana answered. "But I'm makin' this stick. Now get goin'."

IV

The faint, gray flush of dawn showed in the east when Ace Doolin's paint gelding plodded patiently into the large corral that stood below the ranch house of the Bar Z. Ace was slumped forward in the saddle, his head hanging weakly above the gelding's withers. Two other jaw-branded Bar Z horses loomed up out of the shadows to stand beside Ace's horse, the unwieldy bulk of the riders lashed across the saddles making the animals misshapen in the half light.

"Ace!" came the choked cry from one of the bound gunmen. "Ace, damn it, wake up! Get me off this jughead!"

Ace stirred visibly, came slowly back to consciousness, realizing that the animal he rode was standing motionlessly. He raised his head, looked vacantly about him for a moment, and gradually picked out familiar objects until there came a full understanding that this nightmare was nearly over. He was weak from loss of blood, but the chill of the crisp air acted as a tonic to clear his befuddled senses. He shouted once, tried to knee his gelding around the corral and up to the house. But the stubborn animal would not respond, so he continued his hoarse croaking until a light appeared in the bunkhouse window and the dark figures of men came running.

When they had unlashed Ace and lifted him from the saddle, he said: "A couple of you rannies head out toward the breaks and pick up the other three. Slippery's bronc' was buckin' like hell, tryin' to shake Slippery off. The other two followed him."

They carried Ace up to the house, meeting Frazer on the way. The two other riders were taken to the bunkhouse, given a drink of whiskey, and put to bed.

Frazer had Ace carried into his office, a small room at the front corner of the large, frame building. He hurriedly lit the lamp, watching while one of the men ripped Ace's shirt away and bandaged his wound.

"Who did this?" Frazer asked.

"Montana Pierce," Ace growled. "He's raided the place up at Bitter Creek, beefed Bill Rowan, and shot up Frank Humphreys and Pete Crowe. Outside of that, he's drivin' off the herd. There were eight or ten of them, maybe a dozen. We didn't have a chance."

"Why didn't Scotty signal you they were comin'?" Frazer asked. "Wasn't he posted at the Narrows?"

"Sure," Ace drawled sarcastically. "Sure, but they got to 'im. Juan Mercado took care of him."

"Is that knifin' spick sidin' Montana?"

"He is"—Ace nodded—"along with some other salty rannies. Gabe Halpin, Peewee Steele, Ben

Tilton, and a few others. Just a pack of your friends, boss."

Frazer paced nervously up and down in front of Ace's chair, his heels clicking on the bare floorboards.

"Well," Ace said finally, "are you goin' to stay here and let him drive off all that rustled beef?"

Frazer stared thoughtfully before him for a long moment. The dull, yellow glow of the lamp on the desk served to accentuate the breadth of his chunky figure and threw along the wall an enlarged, ape-like shadow that was weird. "This is somethin' that calls for thought and not powder smoke, Ace. We'll let Pierce get away with it . . . this once. Maybe next time he'll make a mistake cuttin' in on my game. If he does . . . we'll see," he said ominously.

Ten days later, in mid-afternoon, Montana was riding across the northern edge of Circle W range, heading toward that spur of timber that bordered the Bar Z pasture where Henry Crossan rode herd. The events of the past few days had wrought a subtle change in him. His lean, angular face was lined with an unnatural frown that came from an intense inner weariness for there had been hard riding and little sleep since the raid on Gabe Halpin's old spread.

But there was satisfaction in thinking of what he had accomplished. After the raid in Bitter Creek Cañon, they had driven out of it three hundred head of cattle that showed signs of recent branding. They had spent all the next day driving them through the hills and across the mountains by way of a low pass. Late the same night they had arrived at the Rafter W hill pasture and left the herd in charge of the Wheeler brothers. The next night they had driven off Frazer's herd of fine yearlings from his western-most range, far distant from the Bar Z. As before, the two gunmen who guarded the herd had been lashed to their saddles and taken back to the Bar Z by Ben Tilton.

Then came the most daring threat to Frazer's strength—the raid on Halfway Wells. The wells supplied water to four thousand acres of open range on which Frazer had recently planted his hired homesteaders. Montana's men swooped down on the camp, dynamited the wells, and rode off leaving the dull, orange glow of burning buildings lighting up the heavens.

Frazer called in Sheriff Canby then, and for four days now Montana and his men had watched from afar the aimless wanderings of a posse of Bar Z riders, headed by Canby. Although they had been safe the whole time, there was a constant strain.

Frazer's strength was ebbing, his herds diminishing in the same way as had those of the neighboring ranches on which the Bar Z had secretly preyed for so long. His range around Halfway Wells was useless without water, and the herds that had dotted it were already moving out.

Montana's thoughts were interrupted as he sighted a rider coming toward him, still a speck ahead on the brown-and-green pattern of the level prairie. The sight of the rider pulled him to an abrupt stop while he debated whether or not to ride the half mile north to the safety of the foothills. His eyes, accustomed to distances, studied the bay horse and found about its swinging run something vaguely familiar. Unconsciously he thumbed out the butt of his Colt, deciding to ride on and meet the oncoming horseman. Then came an abrupt recognition of who this was—Betty Walker.

The bay came up fast, leaving behind a plume of dust spreading out in the still, hot air. A surge of excitement hit Montana and he found himself welcoming this meeting. He noted the lithe grace with which Betty sat the saddle, the rhythm of her slender figure seeming to blend in with the powerful strides of the animal she rode. She wore blue Levi's and a tan shirt, and, as she slid the bay to a stop in front of him, her hair took on the burnished gold of the sunlight.

"Howdy, Miss Walker," he greeted, touching the brim of his hat.

She did not answer immediately, but sat eyeing him with a half-quizzical, unsmiling expression. Abruptly she asked: "Why are you doing it, Montana?" The directness of the question startled him, and, while he was groping for an answer, she went on: "I never thought you'd go this way!"

"What way?" he asked.

"To take to the owl-hoot trail! With a price on your head!"

He smiled. "That's something new. The reward, I mean."

"Frazer's offering fifteen hundred dollars for your capture, dead or alive," she told him, her unflinching gaze boldly meeting his.

"Maybe I ought to offer a reward for him," Montana said easily. "We're two of a kind."

"You are not!" she flared. "In a week since I saw you, you've done more harm than Frazer ever did on this range!"

"Harm?" He shrugged. "I reckon Frazer's the only one who has a complaint to make."

"What about Halfway Wells?" she asked him. "Four thousand acres left without water! There were seven small ranches on that land. You ruined them."

"They were Frazer's," he said firmly. "Frazer hired those homesteaders, planted them on what was open range two years ago. In another year he'd have gone through the pretense of buyin' 'em out. It was his scheme to hog more land and drive off the other outfits."

For a moment she looked at him with a certain defiance. "You're being selfish, Montana! You and the rest that ride with you are settling a grudge. What you're doing won't help the rest of us."

"Why should I help?" he queried, laughing scornfully. "Neither you nor any of the rest would trust me. You wouldn't even give me a job."

"It wasn't I who turned you away," she said levelly. "It was Jim."

"Then you . . . ," Montana began, but caught himself.

"I've never believed what they said of you," came her soft-spoken words. "I still don't. You aren't a killer, Montana."

He sat silently, at first unbelieving. Slowly her words took root in his mind and with startling clarity he saw that she believed in him, that she was sincere. Then it was that he understood how blindly he had gone about his selfish mission on vengeance, and that his real wish all along had been to right the wrong done to Clem Walker and his daughter. He had struck at Frazer, not thinking that others besides himself and his men had a grievance against the man. Her words cut in on his thoughts:

"He'll turn all those things against you. You'll be hunted by every rancher around Singletree! If you really want to help, as you say, get some proof against Frazer! But don't keep on with this awful burning, stealing, killing. . . ." A half sob choked off her words as she wheeled the bay around and abruptly rode away.

He watched her until she disappeared behind a low ridge in the distance. Only then did he continue on the trail that would take him to Henry Crossan.

It was with a wild surge of elation that he realized how Betty's words had crystallized his blind thrusts at the Bar Z owner into one definite purpose. Then came the knowledge that she cared!

A seed of a plan grew in his mind, shaped itself into something so daring as to be incredible. He rode onward, twisting the reins over the saddle horn and building a cigarette. To the accompaniment of the creak of saddle leather and the hollow ring of his gelding's hoofs on the bare rock, he weighed the chances of his seeing this new plan through.

V

Two hours after sundown that evening, Ralph Frazer and Ace Doolin sat in the small office of the Bar Z. Frazer occupied the chair behind the desk, facing the outside door, while Ace sat tilted back against the outside wall. Ace was softly cursing his clumsiness at rolling a cigarette, for his right arm was still stiff from the wound Montana had given him.

The Bar Z owner's black brows contracted in a frown. "What's eatin' you, Ace?"

Ace looked up then, seeming to measure Frazer with his glance. "You're goin' soft, boss," came his startling statement. "Why don't you let me gather up the boys and ride out after that coyote?"

Frazer chuckled. "If you held four aces, would you bet the limit and get the counter-jumpers out of the game?"

"No," Ace answered, after due deliberation. "I reckon I'd play 'em close and keep the others in for a grand killin'. But I can't see that you're holdin' four aces this hand, boss."

"I'm not . . . yet! But after Pierce cuts loose a few more times I will be. I'm lettin' him build himself a reputation, Ace. When he has one, there won't be a rancher in these parts who won't side with me to hunt him down. When he's out of the way, we'll be stronger'n ever."

Ace shrugged. "It may work," he said dubiously. "But first I got to see the man who can corral Montana. He's poison."

Frazer's eyes hardened. "Looks to me like you're losin' your guts, Doolin. It looked that way the other day when Pierce made the whole pack of you take water in Singletree."

The grin that crossed Ace's face was a leering one. "You were in on that, too, Ralph. I didn't see you go for leather."

Frazer shrugged, and the look he gave his foreman was inscrutable. "I hire men to make my gun play for me. In case they go yellow, I'll count on my own irons."

The interruption that came was timely. From outside the sound of a horse pounding into the yard echoed loudly.

Instinctively Frazer stiffened, drew his Colt, and laid it on the desk. The door burst open and Henry Crossan stood framed in it, his face dust-covered and streaked with sweat, his Levi's foam-flecked from a fast run.

"Well, Crossan?" Frazer asked, picking up his Colt from the desktop and dropping it into his holster.

"I've got news!" Crossan said, breathing heavily.

"Must be damned important to bring you five miles at this time of the night! You came in a hell of a hurry, too! Come on, what is it?"

Crossan jerked his head in Doolin's direction, raising his eyebrows in a mute query.

Frazer waved impatiently: "Go on, go on!"

"I saw Montana Pierce tonight," Crossan began. "He . . ."

"You what?" Frazer shouted, rising out of his chair. "Where was he?"

"He came up to where I was ridin' above the line camp."

"Was it a raid?" Frazer snarled. "How many head did they get away with?"

"None," Crossan replied. "Montana came up to see me."

Slowly Frazer eased back into his chair again.

"He's wantin' me to ride with him!" Crossan did not look at Frazer as he spoke, but fumbled in his shirt pocket for tobacco and a match. He did not see the glance Frazer flashed at Ace Doolin, nor the look that passed between them.

"You and Montana were pretty good friends, as I remember it," Frazer said significantly.

Crossan nodded. "He's all right, I reckon. But plumb loco for sittin' in a game that's too stiff for him."

"What did you come here to tell me?" Frazer's impatience could wait no longer.

Henry Crossan did not answer until he had lighted his cigarette. When he did speak, his words were flat. "I've come to claim that reward."

Frazer could not hide his surprise. His eyes narrowed and an ugly grimace contorted his face. "I'll pay that reward when I see Montana Pierce in jail!"

"He's yours for the takin'."

"You know where to find him?"

Crossan nodded.

"Where is he?" Frazer asked.

Crossan laughed quietly. "Let's see some of the *dinero* first."

Frazer's face flushed a dull red beneath his tan. "Crossan, you . . ."

"Cut it!" barked Crossan. Then he smiled again. "I reckon we understand each other, Frazer. You see, I don't trust you any more'n you do me. Pay me half that reward now and I'll lead you to Montana Pierce. Pay me the other half when he's in jail."

The thin line of Frazer's mouth was drawn down in a sneer, but as he met Crossan's steady scrutiny, he seemed to sense that here was a man who would take careful handling. Crossan was one of the few men working for him of whom he knew nothing beyond the fact that he was a gunman. Once he had seen Crossan use his Colt, and as a result of that he had hired the man. Frazer's sneer vanished and a wry smile took its place. "You win, Crossan, but I haven't that much money here now."

"Then I'll wait'll you get it," Crossan replied.

"You're . . ." Frazer started to speak in anger, but some inner warning told him that this was not the time for bluffing. He rose, went over to the safe in the corner, and worked the combination. In thirty seconds he straightened up, threw a roll of banknotes onto the desk.

Crossan picked up the money, counted it deliberately, and then put it in the pocket of his Levi's. "Saddle up and come with me," Crossan said. "You, Ace here, and a couple more. Montana won't be hard to take. You see, I've already taken him. Got him laced up tighter'n a tick!"

* * *

Ten minutes later five riders left the Bar Z yard and went at a fast lope over a low ridge in front of the house. Henry Crossan led the way. For two miles he rode point toward the west, the others pounding after him. As he topped a hogback, he slid his chestnut to an abrupt stop.

"You'll find Montana Pierce tied up behind that outcropping at the foot of this slope," Crossan announced. "And I've got a Colt lined at you, Frazer. Just in case you take a notion you want that money back. Montana's down there. Go get him. I'm ridin'!" With that he wheeled the big chestnut around, bent low in the saddle, and thundered off down the far side of the hogback.

Frazer snarled his oath. "Watch out!" he rapped out. "This may be a trap! Circle that rock down there. Stay away from it till you're dead sure of what's in there. Ace, you and Red swing off to the right! Runt, stick with me. Throw lead if you see anything move. Hurry!" He spurred forward and the others spread out.

It was Ace whose shout echoed across to him. "He's there, Ralph!"

The Bar Z ramrod rode in toward the towering mass of rock and was out of the saddle by the time the others came up, bending over a figure that lay in the sand. Even in that light they could recognize Montana's features, could see the ropes that laced his arms and legs.

Frazer dismounted and strode over to look down at him. "You'll look fine at the end of a rope, Pierce."

Montana raised his head. "Where's that double-crossin' coyote . . . ?"

"If you're referrin' to our mutual friend, Henry, he's just ridden away with the reward money I put out for you," Frazer told him.

Ace Doolin leaned over, took Montana by the shirt front, and hauled him to his feet. "There's a cottonwood over at Poison Springs. Let's ride for it."

"Hold on!" Frazer ordered. "He's goin' in to the sheriff!"

"What're you . . . ?" Ace blurted out haltingly.

"We're makin' him stand trial," Frazer said pointedly. "Savvy?"

A grin broke over Ace's thin face and he nodded his understanding.

Frazer took on the confidence of a man who has finally topped his last obstacle. All the greed for power and success mounted up within him as he stood about, pompously directing his men. They threw Montana over the saddle of one of the riders and headed back for the Bar Z.

"Ace!" Frazer said, pulling in alongside his foreman. "There's not a damn' thing to stop us now. What did I tell you?"

Ace shook his head. "You got me, boss. He sure played into our hands."

Frazer laughed strangely then, and in that laugh there was a sinister cruelty that made even Ace shudder.

VI

The moon edged up over the far horizon as the Bar Z riders neared Singletree with their prisoner. In the clear light the adobes of the town were thrown into gaunt relief, the rounded bulk of their low walls with protruding *vigas* making them look strangely like a colony of fat, overturned beetles. Faint shadows hung in the fog of dust that marked the passage of the riders as they turned into the street and moved on toward the jail.

Montana rode between Ace and Frazer, sitting the saddle with his wrists bound to the horn. As if by mutual consent they had made the ride in silence. Montana had looked behind him only once, and that for the purpose of counting the eight Bar Z gunmen who completed his guard. It was evident that Frazer was taking no chances with his prisoner.

The only lights showing along the deserted street were in the sheriff's office and the saloon. Frazer dismounted before the jail, threw his reins over the hitch rail, and walked over to unlace Montana's wrists.

"Don't be damn' fool enough to try a break," he grumbled as Montana swung stiffly to the dusty street and followed him across the walk and up the steps to the sheriff's office. They found the door open, the office empty, with the lamp on the desk casting a circle of yellow light over the meager furnishings.

In addition to the desk there were three chairs, a safe, a bench along the back, and several reward notices tacked onto the bare walls of the room. An alarm clock ticked off the seconds with a tinny, monotonous sound, its hands indicating the hour to be two-twenty.

Frazer stepped to the steel door at the rear of the office, tried to turn the handle, but found the door locked. As soon as Ace came in, he said: "Send someone up to Canby's house and tell him to come down here with the keys."

While Ace relayed the message to one of the others outside, Frazer stepped to the desk, pulled open the drawers, and went through them. Finally he straightened up and came over to Montana and snapped a pair of handcuffs over his wrists.

"You're playin' me pretty safe, Frazer," Montana said, grinning broadly.

"I'm playin' to see you swing with your neck in a noose tomorrow," came Frazer's ready answer.

"You've played 'em close all along, haven't you?"

Frazer took a seat in Canby's chair behind the desk before replying. "If you knew me better, you'd know I never play 'em any other way." Frazer leaned back, hands laced over his stomach, casually surveying Montana. There was about him an air of supreme confidence as he shifted, reached into his vest pocket for a cigar, and bit off the end of it. His eyes did not leave Montana as he lit a match and drew the smoke of his cigar down into his lungs with evident relish. A low chuckle issued from between his parted lips and he said softly: "You damn' fool, you."

Ace came across the room and sat on the edge of the deck, one foot swinging idly as his cursory glance ran over Montana.

"Supposin' I'd called Canby out to see that wet beef we found up at Gabe Halpin's place the other night, Frazer," Montana said. "You'd have had some tall explainin' to do."

Frazer shrugged carelessly. "What do you suppose I pay Canby for?"

"So you *do* pay him?" came Montana's question, his brows contracted in a look of seriousness. "Careful what you say, Frazer. I might spill a few things at my trial tomorrow . . . if I'm to have a trial."

"You'll get a trial, right enough," Frazer said softly, his gray eyes glinted coldly with amusement. "Only there won't be anyone who'll believe a word you say. Tomorrow's my day, Pierce, and I'm makin' the best of it!"

Montana was silent for a moment. As he lifted his shackled hands to his shirt pocket for his tobacco, he flashed a glance at Ace, saw the frown on his lean face as he regarded Frazer. It was what Montana wanted. He spoke again: "When I'm out of the way, you can run hog wild on this range, eh?"

"Why not?" Frazer replied arrogantly, a low chuckle shaking his frame. "Two years from now the

Bar Z brand will be runnin' across three counties along the foot of the Antelopes. There's nothin' to stop me."

"Careful, boss," drawled Ace. "You'll be sayin' somethin' out of turn."

"Careful, hell!" Frazer snapped, leaning forward in his chair. "What does it matter what he hears? Who's goin' to believe what an outlaw says? You've built your own hang noose, Pierce! When you dynamited Halfway Wells, you made an enemy of every rancher on the range. Your word won't count any more. Even your friend Crossan went against you . . . turned you over for a reward."

"Crossan's a dirty sidewinder!" Montana exploded, then relapsed into silence for a moment, seeming to be trying to get control of his temper. "But at least you've lost out with your fake homesteaders. You lose four thousand acres."

Frazer raised his hands in a matter-of-fact gesture. "It may slow me a year or so. But that water'll come back. I'll put more men out there next year and buy it eventually."

"Ralph, dammit, hold on! You're sayin' things!" Ace's warning came again.

"Hobble your tongue, Doolin," Frazer snarled, banging his fist on the desktop. "It's my own damned business what I say here!"

Ace muttered something unintelligible under his breath, and sauntered over to the door and stood looking out into the night. It was plain that he had no liking for the turn the conversation had taken.

"That was a hell of a trick you used in framin' Clem Walker," Montana said bluntly. "A hell of a trick."

"You broke with me over that, didn't you?" Frazer asked. "Too damned chicken-hearted to back me in that play. I could have used you, too," he mused.

Although the air was chill, beads of perspiration stood out on Montana's high forehead. He shifted a little in his chair with nervousness. "That was too raw," he said, emphasizing his words with a look of loathing. "It wouldn't have worked with anyone but Clem . . . a stranger!"

"I counted on that," Frazer said, seeming to find a satisfaction in divulging his misdeeds. "No one here knows or cares much about Walker."

"So you made a rustler out of him."

"I need that Circle W water. It was easy plantin' that herd. Ask Ace! He helped drive it!"

Ace shrugged his disgust without turning.

At that moment a key grated in the lock of the door behind Frazer. He was turning in his chair to search out the noise when the door swung open and disclosed Peewee's huge bulk framed in the opening. For an instant Frazer hesitated before his hand dropped to his Colt. In that split-second interval Montana lunged, swept the lamp off the desk to the floor.

Behind Montana two deafening shots blended together, and in the light of those gun flashes he saw Ace's .45 sweeping upwards. Montana threw his entire weight into the vicious downsweep of his manacled hands and heard the snap of Ace's wrist as the connecting chain hit it. Ace shrieked horribly, and Montana caught the six-gun as it flew outward from the impact.

He whirled, sent a snap shot in Frazer's direction,

turned back toward Ace just as the Bar Z ramrod's left hand stabbed upwards from his left thigh. Ace fired, the gun flash blinding Montana and sending a searing burn along his scalp as the slug grazed him. Then Montana thumbed the hammer of his Colt viciously, felt the solid buck of it in his hand. Ace's lean frame crumpled and fell forward out of the moonlit doorway.

Outside, someone yelled, and Montana heard men running across the boardwalk and up the steps. He braced himself, standing in the center of the room, and raised his shackled hands to throw two deadly shots at the figure of a Bar Z gunman who suddenly sprang into the doorway.

A crash of glass blended with the shooting outside as someone moved alongside Montana and kicked out a window. His hopes rose, as he sensed the presence of the others in the room. The next instant the place was a roaring inferno of beating gun blasts. Rand Avery's lean figure was outlined a moment at the window as he gunned down into the crowd of Bar Z riders at the foot of the front steps.

The gunmen whipped a hail of lead in through the doors and windows. Montana stepped near a window, peered around the frame, and caught a fleeting glimpse of a man running behind the hitch rail. Montana's Colt sent a purple flame stab into the night, and the runner sprawled on his face.

Montana lingered there a split second too long. A slug tore along his right shoulder as he raised his hands again. A burning stab of pain low in his chest took his breath for a moment. He thumbed his Colt once more, but the hollow click of the hammer told him it was empty. In a sudden frenzy he moved away from the window, slowly for it seemed his muscles had lost their co-ordination.

The stench of powder smoke was strong in the air and bit into his eyes, blurring his vision. All at once a weakness caught him, dragged him down, and he pitched his length across the floor. He tried to cry out, but a blackness blotted his vision. . . .

Peewee Steele's face took form as the fog of unconsciousness cleared from Montana's brain. Montana saw that Peewee was grinning, that his lips were moving. It was an effort to look about, but he did so, seeing that he was lying in bed in a small, neatly kept room.

Peewee's words came to him then: ". . . You've been a hell of a long time comin' 'round, badman! We figured for a while you might be ridin' herd on the clouds."

It came to Montana that Peewee was telling him that he was sick, that he had narrowly escaped death. "How long have I been here?" he asked feebly.

"Just since mornin'," Peewee told him.

A flood of memory left Montana with a mounting curiosity. "Did we get Frazer?"

Peewee's broad grin disappeared. "We got him," he said haltingly. "He was shot up bad so we put him on one of the cots in a cell. Sawbones Yates wouldn't let us move him. That was this mornin'. Well, about an hour ago a mob busted in and took him away." He paused significantly, his face drawn and gone a little pale.

Montana could guess the rest. With a sudden recollection he blurted out: "Where was Canby? Why didn't he have a guard over the jail?"

"The sheriff blew the top of his head off this mornin'," Peewee explained. "Grabbed Juan's cutter and did it before we could stop him. I reckon he saw what was comin'."

After a moment, Montana said: "Was Jim Early in on it?"

"Yeah. Henry Crossan rode out to get him after he'd first taken Frazer over to find you. Told him he'd have to come in to be a witness to a confession. Jim didn't want to miss out on his sleep so he told Henry to get someone else. Henry pulled his iron and brought Jim in anyways. He heard the whole thing from behind the cell-block door. When Frazer told about framin' Clem Walker, I thought he was goin' to claw his way right through that door."

"Henry did a good job, Peewee."

"He's shakin' like a quakin' aspen right now. Said he'd cut his throat if you cashed in your chips. He feels sort of responsible for startin' the whole thing. He was like a loco steer, waitin' there in the jail before Frazer showed up with you. Said he didn't see why Frazer wouldn't beef you when he found you all trussed up an' waitin' for him."

"Frazer had to play it big, Peewee," Montana said. "Bringin' me to trial would have made him the big augur around here for good, and he knew it." He paused a moment, then asked: "How about the rest? Any charges against any of us?"

"Not a one! Gabe Halpin gets his spread back. Clem Walker's out of jail. Hell, there's talk of runnin' you for sheriff! There's others...." Peewee's words trailed off as he stepped backward to look out of the door into the next room. He grinned broadly as he turned to Montana and said in a low voice: "Here comes someone who wants to see you bad."

Almost before he had finished, Betty Walker came into the room. She stood beside the door for a moment as Peewee awkwardly edged his bulk out through it. For the space of two full seconds she stood there, her loveliness filling Montana with a longing he could not keep from showing in his eyes. Then, abruptly, she came to him, knelt beside the bed, and buried her face at his shoulder, sobbing softly. Presently he took her face between his hands and kissed her.

"I'll never turn you away again, Montana," she said at last, and the smile that sparkled in her eyes told him more than a thousand words.

Bondage of
the Dark Trails

The author's original title for this story was "Lawmen Make Mistakes." It was completed in the middle of April, 1937. It was submitted to Popular Publications' Western pulp magazines on May 3, 1937. It was purchased on June 28, 1937 and the author was paid $141.30. The story appeared as "Bondage of the Dark Trails" in *Star Western* (10/37). For its appearance here, the author's typescript has been used for the text but the magazine title has been retained.

I

The man at the stamp window, happening to look out at Sheriff Henry Wallis just then, asked worriedly: "Bad luck, Hank?"

The lawman glanced up from the letter he was reading, the weathered brown of his long face turning a shade lighter, to an unhealthy tan. The muscles along the line of his jaw were corded to erase his usual expression of mildness. "I didn't know for a minute, Bert. No, I don't reckon you'd call it exactly bad news."

But, as he folded the letter, stuffed it in his vest pocket, and left the post office to head up the street, several of the loungers along the awninged walk stared curiously at him. There was a certain grimness in his set expression they didn't often see, and his honest brown eyes, usually pleasantly reflecting the man's inner well-being, were now hard and flinty-looking.

A few doors below the jail, Hank reached out to stop a towheaded youngster running past.

"Have you seen Martha Brill, Davie?" he asked.

"She's over at the grocery with Brace Hardy, Mister Wallis. You want her?"

Hank dipped his hand into his pocket and brought out a dime, handing it to the boy.

"Hike over there and tell her to come to my office right away. Tell her to come alone."

Hank waited until the youngster had started across the street before he walked on to his office. He went in through the open door and stood at the window, his Stetson pulled low over his eyes to shade them against the bright sun glare. He stared impatiently across the heat-shimmering, dusty street at the row of low adobes opposite, until at last Martha Brill came out of the grocery.

At sight of the man who sauntered along at the girl's side, Wallis muttered a sharp oath. He hated Brace Hardy—hated the thing about the man that made him wear black broadcloth and white shirts and fancy-stitched boots when waist overalls and denim shirts and plain boots were good enough for almost every other cattleman on this range.

Hardy's guns, too, reflected his character; they were pearl-handled and hung low in tooled holsters. Pretty as they were, Hank was thinking, the man knew how to use them.

He went on back to sit in his chair behind the desk, and was sitting there a half minute later when the two of them appeared at his doorway.

The girl glanced at him, smiling, saying as she stepped inside: "Something important? Are you joking, Henry?"

"No." Hank shook his head soberly. "But didn't Davie tell you to come alone?"

Martha stood, blank-faced and speechless, at the bluntness of the lawman's words. But Brace Hardy's ebony-black eyes flashed a look of hostility and his broad, squarish face took on a mirthless grin. "Don't worry, Hank. I don't want to stay any more'n you want to have me." He looked down at the girl and added more mildly: "I'll be outside."

As he turned to go, Martha reached out and took him by the arm, saying to Wallis: "Anything you have to say to me can be said in front of Brace."

"If Brace had a right to listen, I wouldn't mind, Marty," Hank said, a strange gentleness in his tone. "But it is personal."

"Personal or not, Brace has a right to hear," Martha countered. "We're to be married."

Hank tried not to be surprised, but he was. He had been expecting this, dreading this, for months. Yet to hear Martha Brill say it took a little of the heart out of him. Just now, a little of the stubborn anger rose in him at sight of Martha's fresh loveliness; he was even fairly amused at the flashing look of anger that edged her hazel-eyed glance. She was demanding respect for her man of choice and, despite himself, he had to admire her for it.

Then, thinking of the letter and what it meant to them both, he gave a weary shrug of his shoulders, took the letter from his pocket, and handed it to her.

She glared at him defiantly a moment longer before she took out the letter and read it:

H. Wallis, Sheriff,
High Butte, Arizona
I am writing to you post-haste to give the news that Mel Hobart died of pneumonia yesterday in the

penitentiary at Yuma. He made a confession shortly before his death that will interest you. On his sworn statement he told witnesses that he alone was responsible for the killing of a Michael Stoffer in the stage robbery near High Butte four years ago.

Hobart admitted that he had been paid one thousand dollars to leave the evidence that implicated William Poe in the murder. Unfortunately Hobart lapsed into delirium and died before he could name the man who paid him to frame Poe.

In view of the fact that Poe escaped from Yuma more than a year ago, I am writing you in hopes that you may help to locate him. If you succeed in doing this, use this letter as your authority to tell him that he is a free man.

All rewards posted for his arrest have been withdrawn. On behalf of the people of this Commonwealth, I hereby tender him my apologies for this miscarriage of justice.

> *Very truly yours,*
> *Leonard P. Shumway,*
> *Governor*

The letter fell from Martha Brill's hand and fluttered to the floor. A look of unfeigned happiness lighted in her eyes, and then, with a stifled sob, she buried her face in her hands and cried: "It can't be! It just can't . . . !"

Brace Hardy's expression was one of bewilderment. He stooped to pick up the letter and read it, and Hank Wallis saw the gradual change that took the handsomeness from the man's swarthy face and twisted it into ugliness.

At length, Brace threw the sheet of paper onto the lawman's desk. "So they're makin' an honest man of that coyote, are they?" he growled.

Martha Brill had time to jerk her head around and gasp—"Brace, how cowardly!"—before Hank Wallis rounded his desk. He struck Hardy an open-handed blow across the face.

As the slap of his hand against Hardy's cheek sounded in the room, Hank Wallis stepped back a pace.

Hardy's face flushed with quick anger. "Shed that badge and that hardware and take the beatin' you deserve, Wallis!" As Hardy spoke, he was reaching down to unbuckle his own gun belts and swing them to one side, well out of the way.

Hank hesitated, knowing the odds that lay against him. Brace Hardy was thirty pounds heavier than he, and young, and with the strength of two ordinary men. But years of smoldering hatred toward this man wiped out all thought of caution. Hank followed Hardy's example, unpinned his badge, and laid it on his desk before he turned to face the younger man.

Martha Brill uttered a low cry as Brace charged in. But Hank waved her to one side and met the rush with a short, hard blow that caught Hardy alongside the temple. For one fleeting second it looked as though the solid smash of his fist had downed Brace Hardy. Brace lost his footing and went to his knees. But he was up again two seconds later, rushing in with his fists beating down the lawman's feeble guard.

It was over ten seconds later. Hank Wallis lay on his back on the floor, a thin trickle of blood streaming out of one corner of his mouth and down along his chin. Brace Hardy stood over him, fists still doubled, and sneered: "Get up and take some more, Tin Star! I still say Bill Poe's a yellow-bellied coyote."

"Brace!"

It was Martha Brill who spoke. She stood halfway behind the sheriff's scarred oak desk, her face drained of color and a look of smoldering anger in her eyes. Brace turned slowly around to face her, as though aware of her presence for the first time. He looked at her guiltily, then looked away again suddenly.

"That was a coward's trick, Brace," Martha told him in a flat, low tone, yet her eyes were blazing. "You might have thought of me when you said that . . . or have you forgotten that Bill Poe's my friend?"

She waited for answer, but Hardy kept a sullen silence. Behind him, Hank Wallis came up onto his feet and limped over to a chair along the side wall.

"There's only one answer to this," Martha went on. "It's all over with you and me, Brace. I'm glad I found out what I did today. Please leave now!"

She waited, coolly aloof, as Hardy picked up his guns and buckled them on again. Once he turned to face her, as though he would have voiced what lay behind the growing look of fury in his eyes. But Brace Hardy had made one mistake that day, and he wasn't making another. He put on his Stetson and went out the door.

Martha came over and stood in front of Hank Wallis. He had wiped the blood from his mouth, and except for a livid bruise high on one cheek bone he looked none the worse for what had happened.

He glanced guiltily up at the girl and said: "I reckon I lost my temper, Marty."

But, strangely, she was smiling. She shook her head. "No, I don't think you did, Henry. I think you did it on purpose. At least I give you credit for having done it, to show me how mistaken I was. You've never liked Brace, have you?"

"He's not your kind, girl," Hank said levelly. "I hated to see him houndin' you, when I knew you still cared for Bill."

She stared down at him unbelievingly. "You . . . knew? Then why . . . why have you spent the last year driving Bill out of the county? You've . . . "

"I know," he cut in, rising to his feet to take her by the arms. "I have a lot to make up to that man. Up until now Bill Poe has been an outlaw. It was my duty to enforce the law that made him one. But from now on I reckon I'll do my best to make him my friend."

"He'll never be your friend, Henry," the girl said slowly. "And he'll never be mine again, no matter what happens. You've hunted him down, made this last year a living hell for him. As for me, Bill will never forget that I was the one who identified that wallet you dug out of the burned stage four years ago. Without that, he'd never have gone to prison. I . . . I sent him there."

The truth of her words freighted the ensuing silence with a potent meaning. Hank Wallis went over to get the letter. He folded it and returned it to his pocket. "I'm leavin' as soon as I can get my saddle on a horse," he told her.

"Leaving? Where are you going?"

"After Bill."

"You're riding to Rustler's Gap?" Martha asked incredulously. She gasped as she read the answer in his eyes, and added quickly: "You can't go, Henry! They'd kill you!"

"I'd be a prime polecat if I wished the job onto someone else."

"Then I'm going with you."

He shook his head soberly. "You'll stay right here. It's a two-day ride and a man's job. I'll go alone."

She sensed then a depth of meaning behind his words, and held back her protest. Hank Wallis had a debt to pay back; he was paying it the only way left for him.

During the next half hour she helped him, going over to the hotel, and having the cook in the kitchen out back pack his saddlebags with grub. When Hank rode out of town, taking the trail that led to the wavering line of the hills on the far horizon to the west, she tried to put down the feeling that she would never see him again.

II

Next morning Henry Wallis knew where it would happen, and, when he came within sight of the place, he felt fear deep-rooted in him for the first time in his fifty-three years. The sagging weight of the guns at his thighs gave him no assurance now, neither did the five-pointed star pinned on his vest pocket.

He was out of his own county, a full day's ride from High Butte, and to his own knowledge no Arizona lawman before had ever lived to ride through that narrow rock-walled notch on the trail ahead. This was Rustler's Gap, and those towering cañon walls closing in to edge the trail threw up a natural barrier, a deadline for any sheriff or posse. Beyond, somewhere high in the hills, was the hideout that had been the safe haven for the outlaws of this country for as long as a man could remember.

Hank Wallis touched the flanks of his bay mare with blunt spurs, all at once impatient to get this over with. He looked straight ahead, pointedly disregarding the margins of the cedar belt that grew close into the edge of the rocky defile ahead. Then suddenly, as the trail swung in alongside the trees, his horse shied violently. This was it!

Two riders, Winchesters across their saddle horns, spurred out from behind the screen of cedars to block the faintly marked trail. The leaner of the two drawled: "This is as far as she goes. All out!"

"I'm here after Bill Poe," Hank answered, his tone level. But inside he felt anything but calm.

"You ain't the first, lawman!" The lean one grinned. "Bill ain't at home."

"He is to Hank Wallis."

For a space the pair stared at him with an open amazement touching their glances. Finally the second one said: "You wouldn't be this Hank Wallis, would you?"

The sheriff nodded.

"Watch him, Slim," the man muttered to his partner. "I'm goin' to have a try at his irons. If he takes a deep breath, let him have it!"

He prodded his bronco and rode in alongside Wallis, reaching out warily to lift the lawman's guns out of their holsters. As he reined back again, jamming the six-guns through his belt, he drawled: "Now let's be ridin'. Goddlemighty, but Bill will love this."

Half an hour later, seeing the trio coming up the trail toward the slab-shacked little settlement at the head of the cañon, a whiskered oldster standing before Trent Buvid's saloon shouted back over his shoulder: "Someone run up the hill after Bill Poe! And run like hell!"

As Hank Wallis entered the far limits of the makeshift street, a swamper cut out the back door of Buvid's place and ran all the way to a small cabin at the outskirts of the town. The oldster, still standing in the saloon's doorway, managed to catch the eye of one of Wallis's guards as the three were riding past a full minute later.

"This'll do!" the guard called out, turning in at the tie rail. His companion circled the lawman and took a position opposite until Hank was out of his saddle, and only then swung stiffly to the ground with his rifle in the crook of his arm.

"Go on in, Tin Star," he said.

Wallis ignored the jibe as he climbed the steps. The hackles along the back of his neck rose as he sensed the gun muzzles behind lined on him. But his spare frame was erect and his grizzled head held high, and he went in alone.

A lean, flat-hipped man in waist overalls and a brown shirt stood halfway the length of the deserted bar. His hawk-like face was so inscrutably set that only his hard, gray eyes seemed alive.

They shuttled from Hank Wallis's face on down to the empty holsters at his thighs; seeing them, he snapped out: "Give him back his guns."

At the command, Slim stepped in behind Wallis and dropped the six-guns back into their holsters. When this was done, the man at the bar smiled thinly, and breathed: "That's better!"

"I came to talk to you, Bill," Hank said.

Bill Poe shook his head slowly from side to side. "No. No talk!"

"Martha Brill sent me."

For a flashing instant a little of the steel-hardness

went out of Bill Poe's gray eyes. "She sent me up here, too," he drawled. "Or maybe you were forgettin' that."

"She made me bring you a letter," Hank lied, playing his only chance. "I didn't want to come. You ought to read the letter before you do anything else."

Poe considered this for a long moment, finally shrugging his wide shoulders. "Why not?" Then a mirthless smile twisted his lips. "We've got plenty of time." He paused, letting his words carry their inference, adding finally: "Slim, you heard him say he had a letter. Bring it to me. The rest of you watch him."

Slim took the folded envelope Hank pulled from his pocket; he circled wide of the line between the two and laid the envelope at Bill Poe's elbow. Then he stepped back out of line again and drew one of the .45s. Poe waited until that gun was leveled at the sheriff before he picked up the letter and read it.

Hank Wallis, watching him closely, saw that he read the letter through twice, deliberately, as though committing it to memory. Finished, Poe crumpled the page and tossed it into a spittoon on the floor a few feet beyond him.

"It's come a little late, hasn't it, Hank?"

"I don't get you, Bill. You're free."

Bill Poe chuckled softly, and his voice rang brittlely: "Free! You mean I could go back and take up where I left off? Me ... with all my outfit gone ... no friends, no money!"

"You've got Martha!"

Poe suddenly shoved out from the bar, bending forward slightly at the waist so that his hands hung over gun butts. "Damn you, Wallis! Mention that girl again and I'll blow your guts out!"

"For over a year I've hounded your trail," Wallis said, watching the threat in Poe's eyes. "You may hate me, Bill, but you know I wouldn't lie. What I say is a fact, and you can go for your iron as I say it. You've still got Martha Brill."

Poe's fingers moved, spreading claw-like at the involuntary anger that drove him like a white-hot scourge. But then, as abruptly as it had risen, it went out of him and he straightened. "I'll forget you said that, Hank. Why did you come up here?"

"Who else would bring you that letter?"

"You could have sent it in by any one of a dozen others," Poe said. Strangely enough, the look he fixed on Wallis was tinged with admiration. "I'll hand it to you, though, Hank. You've got guts. Maybe this is your dumb way of showin' you're sorry for what you've made of me. But . . . me go home again?" He laughed bitterly, holding out his two hands. "Why, you damn' fool, you want me to go home with what I've learned the past four years? Hank, these paws can do things with guns and cards that you've never seen before. Every glory hunter this side of the border would take the ride to High Butte to have a try at Bill Poe. I couldn't work, because work stiffens these hands. Do you get it? You and that girl have made me good for only one thing . . . you've cast me an' my life outside the law, where there's not any peace, any decent folks, any kind of security."

"You could wear a badge, Bill. The law could use your guns."

Poe's strident laughter echoed across the stillness that held the room. "The law!" he snarled. "The law that cooped me up for three years behind rock walls, to live on sour bread and stinkin' soup! The law that hunted me through these hills for a year, an' finally drove me here. The law . . . !" He clipped off his words, suddenly aware that he was shouting, and waited a brief moment until he regained control of himself. Then he added quietly: "No, Hank. You walk out that door and ride away and forget me, while I'm in the mind to let you. I'll stay up here and play out the hand you and that girl dealt me."

In the silence that followed, Slim and the three others standing at the door to one side of Hank Wallis eyed the lawman. Hank was obviously searching his mind for something to help him, for something he could use to change Bill Poe's resolve.

At length he said: "Martha made me promise not to come back without you."

"Martha!" Poe growled. He shrugged helplessly, as though unable to put his feeling for Martha Brill into words. "You go back and tell her to marry that stuffed-shirt, Brace Hardy! Tell her to settle down and raise his kids and spend his money and have a good time! And tell her to forget about me. Because, by God, I've forgotten her!"

"That's a lie, Bill! You haven't forgotten her. She hasn't forgotten you. Five minutes after she'd read this letter, she told Brace Hardy she was through."

Oddly enough, those watching the pair saw that Bill Poe took the words without the trace of an emotion. He shook his head and said soberly: "She can't do without Brace Hardy. He's loaned her dad money. His money saved old man Brill's bank last summer during the drought. If Hardy wants to, he can ruin Brill. Hank, let the cards lay. Get out!"

"There's one more thing I want to. . . "

"Get out, I tell you!"

Hank Wallis had walked into this room a man who carried his years well, a man proud and unafraid and master of himself. But now, as he turned and strode to the door, his steps were the shuffling ones of a broken man. Bill Poe, seeing this and watching the sag to Wallis's square shoulders, smiled mirthlessly, enjoying the moment.

At the door, the lawman faced about and looked back once more. "Think it over," he said. "And if you change your mind, ride down and see me. I'll do everything a man can to square things."

"Thanks, Sheriff!" The two words held the bitterness of a taunting rebuke.

Wallis went on down the steps, staring sightlessly ahead. When he rode back down the trail, he sat slumped in the saddle, not even noticing that two riders followed him to see that he went out through the gap.

It took Hank Wallis longer to ride back to High Butte than it had taken him to come. The fast-settling dusk of the following day saw him ride past the first squat adobes of the town. Martha Brill, waiting for him at the end of the street, had her answer even before he saw her there in the half light.

He reined over to her and sat, looking down and trying not to see the pain that showed in her hazel eyes. Finally he nodded, saying lifelessly: "I did all I could."

"I knew you would, Henry. Don't tell me about it

yet. I want to be alone. Go to your office. Dad's waiting there for you."

For the first time, it struck Hank Wallis as a strange thing that he could be so engrossed in the affairs of these two. Martha Brill had always been his friend; she was one of the very few who never addressed him by his nickname, and in this show of respect he always read her high regard for him. And Bill Poe had once been his friend. He had been glad for both of them, years ago, when everything pointed to their being married.

It had pleased him to see Bill replace Brace Hardy in the girl's affections. But then this had happened, and the duty of arresting Bill Poe had made a harder man of Hank. Now that Bill and Martha had the chance of coming together again, he had failed to bring it about. He felt as if he had failed in the greatest challenge, the greatest chance, that life would hold for him.

As he rode on down the street, he was thinking these things. He had pulled in at the hitch rail in front of the jail before he saw the shadowy figure on the walk and then remembered Martha's telling him that her father would be there waiting for him.

" 'Evenin', Tom," he said, as he climbed down out of his saddle.

"Any luck?" Tom Brill asked, as he followed Hank into the office and took the chair by the wall beneath the board where the lawman had tacked up his Reward posters.

"No luck. What's on your mind?"

For a full ten seconds Tom Brill sat there, not answering, and only then looked up and seemed to push some thought far back in his mind. "It's the

bank. I reckon you haven't heard. The railroad trestle across Willow Gulch was dynamited today. A
gold shipment from Stacey Blair's mine is comin' in
on Number Five in the mornin'. It'll be stored in my
vaults until the trestle is repaired and they can send
it on to Benton."

"The trestle dynamited?" Hank was incredulous.
"Who the hell would do that?"

Brill shrugged. "They don't know. Brace Hardy
and a few others are up there now, tryin' to pick up
sign and ride down the ones who did it. It's no use.
There isn't a man livin' who could track an eight-
team ore wagon more than a quarter mile across
that rock up there."

Hank considered this, nodding grimly. "We can
get that settled later. What about this gold, Tom?
What do you want me to do?"

"Tomorrow's Saturday. The shipment arrives at
six in the mornin'. Give me four deputies to watch
the bank until closin' time. After that, I'm havin' old
Walt Travis stand guard. I reckon it'll be safe
enough. Maybe they'll send a stage over from Benton Monday and take it off my hands."

"There's nothin' to worry about," Wallis said, unable to discover what had put that worried frown on
Tom Brill's face.

"I know, Hank. But I'm spooky tonight. I spent
most of the day talkin' to Brace Hardy. He'll stay
with me only long enough for me to dig up some
money to take the place of what he's drawin' out.
He's madder'n a new-skinned rattler over what
Martha done."

"So that's it." Hank stared pensively at his friend
for a brief moment. "Tom, you're gettin' old. Is there

any reason why me and Wes Rankin and Harry Moss and a few others can't scrape together enough money to tide you over? Forget about Brace. Hell, you knew what kind he was without this havin' to come up to show you?"

Tom Brill was about to answer when the dust-muffled hoof pound of a fast-ridden horse echoed out from the far end of the street. "That'll be Brace now," Tom said.

They waited as the rider came nearer. Then they heard the creak of leather out front as a man swung out of a saddle, and a few seconds later Brace Hardy's wedge-shaped frame was outlined in the doorway. He stood there, regarding the two of them silently for a second or two, and then reached up to push his black Stetson high on his forehead.

"Where's Bill Poe?" Hardy asked.

"He didn't come back with me."

"You're damn' right he didn't!" Brace flared. "He and his wild bunch had somethin' else to do today. Jeff Harmstead, the nester livin' at the foot of Willow Gulch, saw the bunch that dynamited the trestle. He had a good look at a tall gent forkin' a big palomino stallion. Bill Poe rides a palomino."

"Bill Poe didn't do this," Hank said hoarsely, rising halfway up out of his chair. But he sat down suddenly, unsure of himself in the face of Hardy's news. He was remembering that taunting—"Thanks, Sheriff!"—that had been Bill Poe's parting words. And now he knew that Poe could have done this as well as any other man. He and his wild bunch could have ridden out through Rustler's Gap and dynamited the trestle. Was this Bill's way of evening the score with him? Had he known that the gold was coming through the next day on his way to the bank at Benton?

"Bill Poe could have done it," came Brace Hardy's accusing words. "He isn't comin' back, is he, Wallis? He told you to go to hell. This shows you how he stands!"

"You're wrong, Brace," Tom Brill spoke up. The words themselves were intended to show the man's disbelief in what Brace said, but they lacked certainty.

"You two can think what you like," Hardy said flatly, "but I'm seein' to it that the bank is safe. Hank, I want you to put a guard on it as long as that gold's here. Tom, you and I are through! Get that money by next week, or by God I'll close you up!" Brace stood there, glaring at the pair of them, and then turned on his heel and went out.

"We'll have plenty to do these next few days," Tom Brill said. "Hank, it's a funny thing, but I'm glad I'm finished with Brace Hardy."

III

The gold came in on Number Five the next morning at six o'clock. Hank, his deputies posted around the building and the gold locked in the vault, came out of the bank and started up the street for his breakfast. Then he happened to look across and see something in the vacant lot that made him stop abruptly.

A heavy wagon stood at the rear of the lot, piled high with boxes and long planks. A team of gaunt bay geldings was staked out in a patch of grass ahead of the wagon, while halfway beyond it toward the boardwalk a bearded, dusty-overalled oldster was busy spreading out a bundle of canvas.

Hank crossed over and went up to the man, asking gruffly: "What're you puttin' up here?"

The oldster looked up at him from where he knelt beside his canvas. His narrow-lidded, watery blue eyes were touched with a stridently belligerent look until he saw the star on Hank's vest. Then he gave a toothless grin and croaked: "Shootin' gallery, Sheriff. Two-Finger McHenry's shootin' gallery. Me, I'm Two-Finger McHenry. Ain't you never heard of me?"

"No," Hank snorted, looking over the oldster's outfit. "A shootin' gallery? Who in tarnation hell would shoot in one? The boys around here get their practice knockin' tin cans off fence posts. Besides gettin' no business, Two-Finger, you've got to have a permit from the town council to set up a business here. You'd better load up those things and hitch your nags and clear out. I got plenty of trouble on my hands without this."

Two-Finger McHenry thrust a grimy, gnarled fist into an upper pocket of his frayed vest and pulled out a letter. "Here's my permit, Sheriff. Got it yesterday afternoon when I druv in. I'm stayin' right here. I reckon I know my rights!"

Hank read the letter, saw that it was signed by Harry Moss, president of the council, and said: "Go ahead. But don't let the boys tear the town up."

He stayed close to the bank all that day, until closing time, when Walt Travis relieved the four deputies and took up his station with a double-barreled shotgun. As Hank was walking up toward his office, he met Brace Hardy.

"If I was sheriff of High Butte, I'd be ridin' up Willow Gulch to have a look around and talk to Jeff Harmstead," Brace said pointedly. "Or are you afraid you'll find somethin' against Bill Poe up there, Wallis?"

Hank's eyes blazed with an impotent fury as he answered: "You aren't sheriff, Brace. And if there's anything to be found against Poe, I'm not afraid to find it. I'd hang the man if he deserved it. Now get away from me before I lose my temper."

Hardy laughed and went on down the walk. But he had planted the seed of a thought that sent Hank to the livery barn to saddle his horse.

In less than twenty minutes he was riding out the trail east, headed for Willow Gulch. It was a twelve-mile ride and he had all night to make it in. He took his time, finding that to be alone settled his seething thoughts and gave him the chance to reason things out.

Two hours later, when the full darkness had settled down over High Butte, two strangers rode in from the west. One of them, the smallest, had a young and sensitive face and snow-white hair. The other, older and bigger and tougher-looking, had the line of a scar running down the lobe of his left ear to the point of his square jaw.

Coming abreast of Two-Finger McHenry's shooting gallery, Whitey and Scarface reined in and watched the shooting for a few minutes. There was quite a crowd gathered there, filling the walk and spilling out into the street; it was a boisterous crowd, one that booed and hissed and shouted and gasped at the exhibitions put on by the local talent.

The cañon of the street echoed with the thunder of .45s as man after man took his place at Two-Finger McHenry's counter and tried his guns at the targets. This was an occasion; men who hadn't had their guns out of holsters in six months or better lined up and paid their half dollar for ten shots at the clay birds, rabbits, and dogs lined in tiers at the back of the tent.

Even Walt Travis, the guard across the street at the bank, was interested in what was going on. Every five minutes he'd make his circle of the bank and then return to his post, which was atop a rain barrel in the narrow passageway that was between the bank and the adjoining building. There he could be well hidden and still stand high enough to see over the heads of the crowd and into the gallery.

It was nine-thirty when two cowpunchers from Brace Hardy's Wishbone crew blasted away at the only remaining row of targets. When these had spattered back against the sheet-iron back stop, Two-Finger McHenry held up a hand and shouted: "That's all, gents! Unless you'd like to have a try at the wheel. It ain't for beginners!"

His full stock of targets lay in a sloping pile of broken clay shards and white dust behind the stands at the end of the long tent. But there still remained one thing to shoot at. This was a large, twelve-spoked wheel; the spokes continued on through the wheel rim to form pegs, and on the pegs were fastened white clay pipes. Two-Finger McHenry had hired a youngster to stand outside the tent and turn the crank that spun the wheel, and so far the kid had had an easy job. A few had tried shooting at the pipes, only to give it up. It was a hard shot.

"Step up, gents!" Two-Finger McHenry shouted insistently. "The fun ain't over! Hell, ain't there anyone can knock down two pipes off that wheel? Break two pipes and you get your money back, gents!"

Unwilling to ignore his invitation, the two Wishbone riders at the counter reached in their pockets and laid down two more half dollars. Two-Finger McHenry smiled wickedly, bawled an order on back to the kid at the crank, and the wheel started its slow clockwise turning. The two cowpunchers emptied their guns at it, but when the inferno of sound suddenly broke off into momentary silence, all the pipes were still on the wheel.

The two gave up, grinning sheepishly as the crowd behind roared in strident laughter. Still the wheel spun, and still the laughter rose, when suddenly the staccato blast of a six-gun from out on the street commenced its thunder.

Before the astonished gazes of the crowd, five of the pipes on the wheel were blasted into bits that flew outwards to hit the tent wall. The crowd, to a man, crouching now under the hail of lead that sang over their heads, turned to stare in bewilderment at the man who had done this.

He stood in the bed of a spring wagon at the tie rail across the street in front of the bank. He was spare-framed and the most noticeable thing about him was his pure white hair showing below the brim of his wide Stetson.

He got down out of the wagon and came across the street. The crowd melted back to open a line for him, and, as he sauntered up to the counter, another man fell in alongside him. It was Scarface.

The pair didn't walk any too steadily; their walk was a weaving stride, and in less than half a minute the word had spread that these two strangers had been at Bill Finnegan's bar since eight o'clock and were drunk as two loco steers.

Slapping a gold piece onto the counter, Scarface hiccoughed: "I'll use this up. Get that wheel to turnin', oldtimer."

In the next ten seconds the crowd out front saw a thing that had never before met their eyes. The wheel turned, fast this time. And with a smooth and practiced ease Scarface snaked out a gun and emptied it in one continuous thunder; and then, so fast that the eye couldn't follow, he flipped up his other gun, crossed it to his right hand as his left caught the empty, and continued the blasting until ten pipes were missing from the wheel.

The only sound that followed was the dull click of the ejector of Scarface's .45 as he pushed out the empty cartridges. He had reloaded one of his weapons and was turning his attention to the second, when Two-Finger McHenry came out of his stupefied silence.

Looking out at the crowd, he protested: "Don't someone else want to try?" Scarface turned and echoed in a voice obviously thick with whiskey: "Yeah! What's the matter with you jaspers? Step up and show us some lead-slingin'."

A dead silence greeted his challenge. He smiled thinly, as did his companion, Whitey. Then he drawled: "All right! The bunch of you clear out! I'm havin' a little practice here, and I don't aim to make it a free show!"

He waited. The crowd backed away a little. But to men who have lived all their life with guns and who admire good shooting, what was coming was a thing they all wanted to see.

Scarface thought differently. "I said to clear out!" he commanded. Abruptly, to emphasize his words, the gun in his hand blasted flame. A man at the edge of the crowd howled and ran up the street and those who had seen the spurt of dust the bullet made at his feet followed after him. The others were slower to break, but in ten seconds they realized that Scarface was serious about wanting to be alone.

The street cleared.

Scarface and Whitey were drunk and having a little fun, all of Two-Finger's targets were shot up anyway, and this was Saturday night. Why let a couple drunks spoil the evening?

Walt Travis, across the street and standing on his rain barrel alongside the wall of the bank, was the only one besides Two-Finger McHenry who saw that exhibition of fancy shooting. He forgot his duty as guard, and glued his eyes to the spinning wheel across the street. Time and again Two-Finger McHenry had to replace those clay pipes.

Travis wasn't close enough to hear Whitey say to Two-Finger: "We're ready!"

At those words, Scarface picked his guns off the counter and faced the wheel. Two-Finger McHenry had put twelve new clay pipes on the wheel. It started turning and Scarface's guns nosed up in a sudden double blast.

Walt Travis watched closely, the inferno of sound beating at his ears. Suddenly he saw the other, Whitey, swivel around with a gun planted at his hip. That gun belched flame, its roar drowned out by the roar of Scarface's .45s. Walt Travis felt the air whip of a bullet fan past his face, and then he was jumping off the rain barrel and diving down the passageway to safety.

His frantic run took him only three steps. A bullet slammed into his back and broke his run and knocked him sprawling on his face. He screamed, but that scream was drowned into nothing by the thunder from the shooting gallery.

The pair across at the gallery moved quickly after that. Whitey crossed the street and into the passageway alongside the bank in full view of at least twenty men who stood along the walks. They paid him little or no attention. Scarface walked up the street fifty yards and then crossed over.

Whitey stooped over Walt Travis's huddled figure only long enough to be sure that the man was dead. Then he went on back and disappeared around the back corner and into the alley.

Five minutes later the blast inside the bank ripped out the front windows and the doors and sent a cloud of dust boiling across the street. In the half minute it took the town to come to its senses, the two strangers came out of the bank's back door, carrying a heavy box and two bulging saddlebags. They hurried down the alley to where their two broncos were tied under a deserted lean-to. Then the cries out front drowned out the thud of their broncos' hoofs as they quartered out from the shadows of the buildings and rode away.

It was a full half hour after the explosion that Hank Wallis rode his lathered horse down the street and pulled up in front of the bank. By that time they had carried Walt Travis's body down to the hardware store and Tom Brill and Martha and a few others were inside going through the rifled vault. Brace Hardy and thirty riders had formed a posse and were riding out after the robbers.

Tom Brill came up to Hank as the lawman entered and told him: "The vault's cleaned out, Hank. Everything gone! Securities, cash, gold . . . everything!"

Martha stood at her father's side with a helpless, stunned look in her eyes. She reached out to hand Hank a crumpled sheet of soiled paper, saying softly: "I found that behind the vault door, Henry. Read it."

The sheriff smoothed it out in his palm and looked at it, unbelieving. It was the governor's letter he had taken up beyond Rustler's Gap to deliver to Bill Poe!

Inside Hank something balled up his guts. At first he wouldn't let himself believe the glaring truth of this evidence, but after sober thought he couldn't deny it. He looked down at Martha, and said quietly: "We were wrong about him."

She nodded, tears filling her eyes, and turned away from him. For the next ten minutes Hank worked off his inner rage by helping the others to clear away the débris and to force the vault door shut again on the few things of value left inside. Then he and Martha and Tom Brill went down the street to the jail office. For the next hour they sat there in a heavy silence, waiting for Brace Hardy to return with the posse.

When the band of riders came into the far end of the street and rode on past the jail, their silence was eloquent. Brace Hardy saw the light in the jail office and swung in at the hitch rail out front. He climbed wearily out of his saddle.

He was a different man as he stepped into the sheriff's office. All his arrogance was gone now, and his eyes no longer flashed that strong hostility as he looked across at Hank and said mildly: "We're in for it. They got away."

His manner was as surprising as the news he brought. They all looked at him with a growing puzzlement touching their glances. He read their unspoken question, and the hint of a patient smile crossed his face as he nodded. "I made a damn' fool of myself yesterday, actin' the way I did, Brill. This is no time for me to pull out on you. I'll wire the bank at Phoenix tomorrow. Maybe I can scrape together enough to see you through."

It was a full ten seconds before anyone could speak in the face of this bewildering change in the man. Brace Hardy, of all men, to be offering an unmistakable apology!

Martha Brill spoke finally; she looked at Brace as though seeing him in a strangely new light: "You mean . . . you mean you're going to help us, Brace?"

"Yes. This other, this about Bill Poe . . . well, it couldn't be helped, I reckon." He shrugged his thickly muscled shoulders in a show of resignation. "I'd be a prime polecat to let a thing like that interfere now."

Martha rose from her chair and crossed the room to stand in front of him. She was smiling a little as she said: "Can you forget the things we said to each other, Brace? Can it go on as though Bill had never come between us? I . . . I'd like it to."

He nodded soberly, reached out to take her by the arms, and leaned down to kiss her forehead. Her color heightened as she flashed an embarrassed glance back at her father and the lawman. Then she stepped around Brace and went out the door. Her father followed her.

Hank Wallis had watched all this, and, as he saw Brace kiss the girl, he frowned. But he waited until Martha had gone out of hearing and then drawled: "What's your play, Brace?"

For a long moment the gazes of the two caught and held in a quick, flaring antagonism. Abruptly

Brace Hardy said: "Quit ridin' me, Hank! Can't a man admit he's wrong?"

For the second time that night Hank Wallis questioned his own judgment. He had been wrong about Bill Poe, and now it looked as though he had misjudged Brace Hardy. He felt suddenly older than ever before in his life. Without answering Brace, he turned back to his desk and picked up the crumpled letter Martha had found in the bank.

"This was lyin' behind the vault door," he said, handing it to Hardy.

Brace looked at it, then across at Hank. "Anyone tryin' to frame Bill Poe could have left this behind."

The look in Hank's brown eyes sharpened at the words. He nodded. "I've been thinkin' the same thing. But damned if I thought you'd mention it. You see, Brace, I've had the idea all along that you're the only one I know who'd like to frame Bill." He paused, studying Hardy until the man's unflinching gaze gave him the answer he sought. Then he almost whispered: "I was wrong about you. Bill Poe wasn't framed."

IV

Toward noon of that day, a rider headed west out of town, his bronco holding a steady trot. No one was particularly interested in his going. A mile beyond town he cast a swift glance back along the trail. Seeing that it was deserted, he beat his bronco's flanks with his spurs and sent the animal into a driving run.

That day, on his way to the hills, he ran the guts out of two horses, and rode a third through Rustler's Gap shortly after dark. Before sunup the next morning, Bill Poe and three other riders came out through the gap and rode down the cañon.

Poe was astride a big-chested palomino stallion. Slim, the guard who had ridden into the hide-out with Hank Wallis, was one of the three who were with Poe now. As they started down the cañon trail, Slim suggested dryly that they ride a little faster.

"We've got the whole day and half the night for this," Poe told him. "I'd rather do my hurryin' at the other end."

He held a steady pace, and by mid-afternoon the

low-lying butte that backed the town showed on the far horizon. Almost as they came within sight of it, Poe reined in and sat his saddle, gazing pointedly ahead along the trail. There, hardly recognizable in the distance, showed a team and a heavily loaded wagon crawling slowly toward them.

"That'll be the old jasper with his shootin' gallery. Slim, you keep on up the trail and take a good look at him, just to make sure. We'll circle."

They split there, Slim keeping on at a steady trot down the trail, while Bill Poe and the other two right-angled and rode off out of sight. When they met four miles farther on, Slim confirmed Bill's guess. "He's a gabby old ranny. Told me all about the bank bein' robbed. Said he was headed for Benton."

Bill Poe's lean face broke into a smile as he drawled: "He can't get far. We'll take care of this other first."

An hour before dusk he led them off the trail a good mile and into the bed of a shallow coulée, where they cooked and ate their supper. After they had finished and were rolling their smokes, Bill gave a last word of advice: "Remember how we play it. I don't want to let on to him that we know a thing."

Hank Wallis's jail office window showed a light through the darkness as the four of them walked their broncos into the far end of the street. Bill Poe and Slim turned in at the tie rail fifty yards short of the jail and climbed down out of their saddles. The other pair rode on past and reined in at a like distance beyond it.

Slim crossed to the opposite walk and was joined

there in a few seconds by one of the pair beyond; the two of them melted into the impenetrable shadows of the awninged walk and took up their stations directly across from the jail. Bill Poe waited until the remaining man had edged in out of sight at the far corner of the building, and then came down the walk and turned in at the office door.

The lawman sat behind his desk, reading a newspaper. He glanced up obliquely at his visitor, and in the flashing instant of recognition his spare frame became wire-taut. His two hands spread out on the desktop for a moment, as though he was about to push himself up out of the chair, but then, catching the look on Bill's face, those hands relaxed. After a second or two he said ominously: "They've doubled the reward posted for you, Bill. It's dead or alive."

Poe nodded, his smile hardening his expression rather than relieving it. "I got the word last night."

"You got what word?"

Poe took a long moment framing his answer, his face set rigidly in that cold smile. "It won't do, lawman," he drawled. "I have friends here. One of them rode up to me with the news. It was a nice frame-up, only I can't savvy how you thought you'd make it stick."

"Make what stick?"

"Hangin' the job on me," Bill explained. "I know, for instance, that you left town about dark the night the bank was robbed, pretendin' to ride to Willow Gulch. I'm guessin' that you came back and helped Al Hogan and Whitey Emrick do the job. It took a lot of plannin', didn't it? Dynamitin' that trestle up Willow Gulch, hirin' that old jasper to bring in his shootin' gallery, so's Whitey and Al could have a clear play at the bank. Hell, Hank, it's as plain as your two big feet that you did it."

Hank Wallis visibly suffered at the full realization of what Bill Poe was saying. He lunged up out of his chair suddenly, his hand clawing at his gun. But his gesture froze in the face of the perfectly timed draw that pointed Bill Poe's .45 at his hip.

"I ought to cut down on you," Bill drawled quietly. "I would, only I haven't heard enough just yet. Sit down, Hank."

The sheriff hesitated at the deadliness behind the command. He was no coward, but now was no time to lose his head. So he eased back down into his chair.

"No, I haven't heard yet what reason you had for hangin' the blame on me," Bill went on. "Was it because of your damned ornery . . . ?"

"There's one thing you're forgettin'," Hank interrupted. "The letter. How could I have left the letter there to be found?" A flash of color rode across his drawn features as he spoke, for he was realizing how ridiculous it was to be defending himself.

Bill Poe's puzzlement was genuine. "What letter?"

"The one I brought up to show you four days ago. The letter from the governor."

"What about it?"

"Martha Brill found it behind the vault door in the bank after the robbery."

"So she's in on it this time, too?" Bill muttered, his tone edged with stinging bitterness. After considering this a moment, he nodded soberly: "I can see now how you got the letter back. Al Hogan and Whitey Emrick rode in at the hide-out after you'd gone the other day. You must have met them on the way in and told them I'd thrown the letter away. One of them went to Buvid's and got it for you, so you could leave it in the bank. It was a smart play, Hank." His hard, gray eyes were touched with a fleeting look of admiration. "Only it didn't go through. You must be the one who framed me four years ago, too. What did you have against me? I want to find that out before I pull this trigger."

For the space of a full minute, Hank Wallis's belief in his own sanity wavered. Bill Poe either believed what he was saying, or he was playing a part to perfection. Every detail he had given fit perfectly and logically; Hank himself could have planned the frame-up and carried it out. And now once again, the lawman felt a rising doubt as to Bill Poe's guilt. At length, unable to see the answer to the riddle, he protested: "Let's begin over again, Bill. Let's start with this. I didn't frame you, and I don't know who did . . . if it's true you were framed."

"I didn't think you'd talk. You have enough guts to let me wipe you out and still not spill . . . "

"Hold on!" Hank snapped, suddenly cutting in. For the past few seconds he had been trying to recall something Poe had said a minute ago—something he had overlooked that was the key to the whole tangle. Now he had it. He came up out of his chair and reached down to unbuckle his pair of belts. Laying his holstered six-guns on the desk in front of him, he said: "Take these irons, Bill. You've got men out front, haven't you?"

"I'd be a damned fool to ride in here alone." Poe grinned.

"Then take these guns and use 'em on me if I don't play square with you. We're goin' on a ride."

"A ride?" Poe shook his head. "Not with you, Hank. I wouldn't trust you."

"You said a minute ago that I'd framed that robbery with the old jasper who had the shootin' gallery. I didn't, Bill, but someone else did!"

"I don't get it. Is it another trick?"

"No," Hank insisted. "But I let McHenry get away without questioning him. He left this mornin', headed for Benton, so I heard. You and the rest can take me and we'll ride out after him. Goddlemighty, why haven't I thought of this before?"

"You tell me," Bill said, hesitating a moment finally to add: "I don't know what your play is, lawman, but I've got three salty gents out front who love you just about as much as I do. Come on."

Outside, Bill held a whispered conversation with Slim, who had crossed the street as he saw the two of them come out. Slim went down to the livery stable with the unarmed lawman, and fifteen minutes later the five of them were heading back along the west trail.

It took them two hours of steady riding to come to the point where Bill and his men had seen Two-Finger's wagon that afternoon.

"He wouldn't have gone much farther," Bill said, as they reined in and followed Slim who took the lead. Bent low over saddles, they could see the wheel marks in the dusty trail. The stars gave only a faint light, but it was good enough for following this plain sign.

The broad tire marks were plainly visible for all of three miles farther. Then, at a point where the trail climbed steeply up over a long stretch of bare rocky hillside, they lost the sign.

As they topped the rise, Bill reined in and said: "You three swing out and circle this place. The sign's within a half mile of here, or he picked up that wagon and carried it off on his back."

It was Slim who found the wagon. He returned in less than ten minutes to lead them to it. It stood behind huge, weathered boulders on the hill's far side, well hidden from the sight of anyone riding the trail. Near it they found one of Two-Finger's gaunt geldings staked out in a patch of grass.

Bill was watching Hank now. The lawman got down out of the saddle without a word and walked to the wagon. He lifted the tarpaulin cover and looked in under it. Then he came back and looked up at Bill Poe. "McHenry rode that other jughead away from here without even cookin' a meal. What does that mean to you, Bill?"

"It means he rode away. Should it mean somethin' else?"

"Hell, yes, it should!" Hank exploded. "You know what I'm tryin' to say, Bill. Brace Hardy's layout is three miles off there to the north."

The darkness hid Bill Poe's satisfied smile as he drawled: "You're talkin' in riddles, Hank. Tell it to me straight."

"You know what I'm sayin'. McHenry was in on the bank robbery. And my guess is that we'll find him at Hardy's Wishbone. If he's there, I'm going to like it."

Bill turned in his saddle and said to Slim: "Give Hank back his guns. He's got some sense, after all."

Hank took the double belts, and swung them around his waist. He realized suddenly that Bill Poe had planned all this; he had more than a suspicion that things had been maneuvered tonight so that he would find his own answer without having to be told. He smiled a little grimly when he thought of his own bull-headedness. Bill Poe knew him better than he knew himself.

"How long have you known it was Brace Hardy?" he queried.

"Not so long. I always thought he framed me four years ago, but I couldn't prove it. Last night, when I heard about Whitey and Al Hogan robbin' the bank, I was sure they'd been hired by the same jasper who hired Mel Hobart four years ago. Whitey and Al sided Mel before he was sent to Yuma, an' died there. At first I thought about huntin' those two, but I reckon they're below the border by now. There wasn't much else to do but try and find the old gent with the shootin' gallery. It looked to me like he was in on it."

"But what about your story of me framin' you?"

Bill chuckled softly. "Never curb-bit a horse with a sore mouth, Hank. I knew you'd be too riled to listen to what I had to say, so I threw a scare into you."

"It worked," Hank admitted, his tone betraying his ungrudging admiration. "From here on out I aim to be a help."

"Let's be ridin' then," Bill said.

"Not yet. We need proof for this, Bill."

"And how do you aim to get it?"

"We'll wait for Two-Finger McHenry. Chances are he'll be in a hurry to get out of this part of the country. He'll be back shortly. Send your men back along the trail with our bronc's. You and I can wait here."

V

"You can't do this to me!" Two-Finger McHenry croaked, less than half an hour later. Hank and Bill Poe were facing him, and Hank had a six-gun leveled at the oldster. Two-Finger McHenry's bearded face showed itself an ashen color in the faint light as he added feebly: "I ain't done one damned thing ag'in' the law!"

This had gone on for the past three minutes. McHenry was weakening, but not fast enough for Hank, who now turned to Bill and said: "Go back up the trail and tell 'em to light the fires."

Poe started climbing the hill in the direction of the trail when McHenry's strident cry stopped him: "Wait! What fires?"

"There's a lynch-mob on the loose for you out there somewhere, McHenry," Hank told him ominously. "I was hopin' we wouldn't have to light the fires to signal 'em in."

"A mob?" Two-Finger McHenry echoed hollowly. "You'll turn me over to a mob?"

Hank shrugged his shoulders. "I've done all I could. This is out of my hands now. Most of the mob lost money in the bank. I'd be lynched if I let you go."

"Stop!" McHenry bawled, seeing Bill once more start up the hill. "Maybe we can talk this over." He looked at Hank with a faintly cunning light in his eyes. "You still say you'll let me drive out of here if I tell what I know?"

"Sure. But you'll have to be quick about it. I can't tell when that bunch'll come ridin' back here. It's up to you how you get away, McHenry."

"I'll talk," Two-Finger began. "I'll tell you everything I know." His words poured out now, as he suddenly put aside every thought but that of saving himself. "It was Brace Hardy, Sheriff! He's the ranny that rigged up the whole thing! He hired Whitey and Al and me. My share was a pound of dust to come in with him. Hell, that's more'n I make in a year with this outfit!"

"You rode out tonight to collect your share?"

Two-Finger McHenry nodded jerkily, reaching into his back pocket to pull out a bulging rawhide sack. "Here it is, Sheriff. Take it! Take it and let me go!"

"Where's the rest?"

"At Hardy's. He has it in his place somewheres. I know it's there because he didn't go out of the house when he went after my share."

"Can you be out of the county by sunup?"

"I'll be out of the state by noon tomorrow!" McHenry asserted.

"Then pull out. Don't take to the road. You might run into trouble."

They watched him hitch up his gaunted team and drive off into the night, laying his blacksnake whip across the animals' backs so that they lunged against the traces and made off with the rumbling, careening wagon.

Then, half an hour later as the shadowy cluster of buildings of the Wishbone rose up out of the darkness ahead, Hank drew rein and told the rest: "Bill, you trade horses with Slim. There's a bounty on palominos since the trestle was dynamited. You'll come with me, Bill, directly to the house. You other three scatter and cover us."

When Slim and his two companions had ridden off, the sheriff rode in close to Poe and asked: "What about Martha, Bill? I'd like to know before we go into this that it's all right between you two."

Poe sighed audibly. "A man's got to be wrong about some things, Hank. I was about her."

"What I said about her the other day was straight, Bill. She's still thinkin' of you. There's never been anyone else for her. Will you go back after this is over?"

"Let's finish this first before we start thinkin' ahead."

They rode on, straight down the trail to Brace Hardy's big, low-walled adobe house. Hank rode into the yard first, as they'd agreed on. Bill came behind, with his Stetson pulled low on his forehead so that its shadow would hide his face from the watchers that must be there.

The sound of their approach brought a light in one of the windows. Then the orange rectangle of an open door showed for an instant, and a moment later they saw several shadowy figures moving about under the cover of the darkness of the wide porch.

"Anyone home?" Hank called out as he drew rein twenty feet out from the porch.

"Hello, Wallis," came a voice they both recognized as Brace Hardy's. "What brings you here?"

"I'll be damned if I know yet," Hank growled. "I got the idea tonight I'd like to talk to the old jasper who ran the shootin' gallery the other night. McHenry, his handle was. They said he drove out the west road, so I came after him. I lost his sign in that *malpais* on Ten Mile Hill. Thought maybe he rode over here."

"Why would he be here?" came Hardy's voice, edged with suspicion.

"On second thought, I reckon he wouldn't," Hank said. "I figured he might be tryin' to bum a meal. Well, we'll be ridin' for town. I sure hate to lose that old rannihan. How about a cup of java before we leave, Brace?"

"Sure thing. Light down and come up," was Hardy's cordial answer. They could see him now, standing on the top step of the porch. He turned and gave an order to one of his men, and then called out: "Let's go into my office!"

Hank and Bill Poe got down out of their saddles and walked across to the porch and up the steps. Brace Hardy had gone on ahead, opened a door, and lighted a match.

As the two of them followed, Hardy was turning up a lamp on his massive oak desk. He waved Hank to a chair alongside the desk, asking: "Who's with you, Wallis?"

"Bill," Hank said, stepping to one side of the door and ignoring the chair Brace had pointed out.

"Bill who?"

"Bill Poe."

In the space of a quickly drawn breath, Brace Hardy's heavily muscled body took on a set rigidity. His black eyes reflected a surface light that concealed whatever thoughts were crowding up in his mind. He looked sharply at Bill Poe's face, then down at Poe's guns, and with that he was easing himself slowly down into his big swivel chair.

Hank put in just then: "I was wrong about *looking* for McHenry, Brace. We've already talked to him. He's told us all there is to tell."

The cunning look that came to Brace Hardy's blunt face sent a flood of wariness surging through Hank Wallis. He stepped farther from the door while Bill took up his station at the other side of the opening.

"Then you know how the bank was robbed?" Brace queried, his tone surprisingly natural.

"We know you were behind it," Hank answered.

"Maybe you know about the stage robbery four years ago, too?" Brace was looking at Poe now.

Before Bill could make his answer, Hank said: "No. I don't know, for instance, how Mel Hobart got hold of Bill's wallet that was found in the stage."

Hardy's soft, confident chuckle brought Hank edging out farther from the wall. Hardy's eyes were shuttling between the sheriff and Poe now, watching their every move, as he said: "That was easy for Mel. He slipped it out of Poe's pocket the night of the robbery . . . while he bought Poe a drink." He folded his hands on the desktop before him in a gesture that was at once relaxed and natural. "Mel stuck the wallet down behind the seat cushion so it wouldn't burn."

Suddenly, without his glance giving one shade of warning, the fingers of Brace Hardy's right hand snaked up under the cuff of his left shirt sleeve. Poe saw it coming and made a frantic stab at his holstered Colt. But before his hand closed on the gun butt, Hardy had drawn a double-barreled Derringer out of his sleeve and lined it.

As Poe's hand edged away from his weapon, Hardy smiled and added: "It's goin' to be hard to get rid of you both. But it can be done. You'll be found dead out along the trail. It'll look like a shoot-out. My crew won't give me away."

"This place is surrounded, Hardy." Bill Poe was speaking for the first time since entering the room. "You don't think we'd ride in here alone with what we knew, did you?"

For a split second Brace Hardy took his eyes off Hank Wallis and looked fully at Poe, at the man he hated, and in that flashing space of time Hank was moving. He lunged sideways, his two hands blurring to his guns. Hardy suddenly realized his mistake and swerved his Derringer, lunging up out of his chair to cut loose a double blast at the lawman.

Hank's spare frame jerked back in the face of that death charge, but then his two guns were planted at his hips. His thumbs slipped off the hammers and his .45s set up a deafening inferno of sound that seemed to beat the walls outward.

Bill Poe's guns flashed out, but he only lined them unfired at the Wishbone owner, seeing what was taking place. For Hardy's white shirt front now showed a smear of red. The man's weapon fell from his fist and his two hands clawed at his chest. Hank Wallis cut loose again, and Hardy's two hands suddenly became a bloody pulp as the lead slugs whipped into them. He screamed, but his terrified voice was drowned out by gun roar. For a long moment the look on Hardy's twisted face was one of mingled rage and bewilderment. Gradually his eyes lost their sharp glitter and dulled to a vacant, sightless stare. His arms dropped loosely to his sides, his knees gave way, and he toppled back against the wall to slide slowly to the floor with his shirt now a bloody, torn smear.

Hank, intent on what he had done, failed to hear the running steps on the porch outside. Bill Poe heard them and stepped over to turn out the lamp. An instant later the doorway was lighted with a gun flash and the room was once more beating with a full explosion.

Then, from the night's farther limits, came the double crack of a rifle. The shadowy figure in the doorway groaned once and limped back along the porch. There were startled cries outside now, and a mad scurry away from the office door as three more rifle shots whipped out.

Bill and Hank heard the men outside run to the far end of the porch and around the corner of the building. In the full silence that followed, Bill asked: "Did he get you, Hank?"

"A crease was all," Hank answered.

They waited there in the darkness for all of three minutes. Suddenly, from out behind the building, came the sound of running horses. The hoof pound grew louder and swept on past the building. The two of them went to the door and were in time to see a dozen riders streak out the trail leaving a boiling cloud of dust behind.

"That'll be the whole crew," Hank said. "By sunup they'll be out of the country. Bill, we did ourselves a job."

"You did, you mean," Bill answered, his voice a little unsteady from an inner emotion.

He struck a match and lit the lamp once more and looked at Hank. The lawman's right arm was hanging awkwardly at his side. With a muttered oath Bill came up to him and ripped away the sleeve to look at the wound.

The muscle of Hank's arm was badly torn and bleeding. Bill made a tourniquet of his bandanna and stopped the flow of blood. Slim and the others rode into the yard as he finished.

"Let's get done with it," Hank said, pushing Bill away. "There's the gold to find now."

It was Slim who finally found the gold and the securities cached under a pile of gunny sacking in an unused storeroom in one end of the house. They packed the gold and Brace Hardy's body on two led broncos and took the trail back.

Yet, as they neared the towering shadow of the outcropping where they had last seen Two-Finger McHenry, Hank Wallis shifted nervously in his saddle and let his thought center on Bill Poe. He wasn't sure of the man, for four years had changed him—hardened him into a character that was beyond understanding.

Hank searched his mind for something to stop what he knew was coming, for he had decided that Bill would be riding back to Rustler's Gap with the others, to take up the life that had been forced on him.

Suddenly Hank had a thought. "Bill," he said, "this arm of mine is through, so far as handlin' a gun is concerned. I'm goin' to be a damn' poor excuse for a sheriff from now on."

"It'll get well," Bill answered.

"No, not well enough for me to do a proper job. I'll have to find a good deputy."

Then they rode on in silence, skirting the hill with the twin ribbons of the road in sight in the darkness up ahead.

When they reached the road, Bill Poe would make his choice. He would either head west toward Rustler's Gap or ride east toward town with Hank. And the lawman was determined not to make that ride home alone tonight.

"I'll have to find me a good deputy," he repeated. "If he's good enough, he'll be elected sheriff next fall," he said. "He should be a married man, steady, honest, and able to take care of himself."

"Got anyone in mind, Hank?"

"No."

They pulled to a halt at the edge of the road. Hank was watching his outlaw friend. Bill Poe sat in silence for a good half minute. Then he all at once reached out to take the lead ropes of the two pack horses from Slim.

"I won't be sidin' you from here on, Slim," he said quietly. He wound the two ropes about his left hand, and added: "Tell the bunch to keep clear of High Butte. There's to be a new deputy in town . . . by the name of Bill Poe."

Ghost of the Chinook

Jon Glidden completed the story he titled "Ghost of the Chinook" in early May, 1938. His agent, Marguerite E. Harper, submitted it to editor Robert O. Erisman at the Red Circle Magazine group published by Manvis Publications on May 31, 1938. The story was purchased on July 15, 1938 and the author paid $45. It was published as "Ghost-Guards Ride the Sunset Stage" in *Western Short Stories* (3/39). For its appearance here, the author's original title and text have been restored.

I

Llano Ackers knew he was licked the day Pat Sewell, his one remaining driver, wanted ten dollars a mile to take a bullion stage the thirty-eight miles from the smelter at Lode to the bank at Butte. He had a lot of things to say to Pat, things he later wished he hadn't said, but he was a stubborn man. Pat was stubborn, too, and it was hard after all those months to realize what the oldster's refusal meant.

Pat's last words were: "Hell, Llano, the money I'm askin' wouldn't any more than pay for buryin' me!"

That grim reminder was the thing that checked Llano's anger, made him say: "Maybe I've been runnin' off at the mouth, Pat." He knew from the look in the oldster's eyes that he was already forgiven.

Because he had never before run up against a thing he couldn't whip with either his six-foot, wide-built frame, his guns, or his brains, he decided to do his own driving that night on the run to Butte. Because he didn't know any man but Pat good enough with a shotgun to trust, he decided to make the trip alone.

Late that afternoon he scrawled a two-line message on a sheet of paper and sealed it in an envelope and paid a youngster a quarter to take it out to Bob Morley at the smelter, promising another quarter when he received Morley's answer. Old Bob's answering message was: *We can try anything once.*

At eight that night, giving Pat a check for the last of his pay, Llano told him: "There's five dollars extra there, Pat. I want to use your team and buckboard tonight."

"You got somethin' in your craw, Llano. What is it?" Pat was frowning.

"Check out of your room at the hotel, tell anyone who wants to know that you're headed down to Butte to look for work. Hitch your team and drive your rig out to the fork that cuts north half a mile from town. Hide the outfit above the forks and take your blankets up into the hills and sleep out tonight. I'll have your rig back at the stable by mornin'." He paused, then added: "And you might leave your Greener under the seat."

Pat leafed a five-dollar bill from his sheaf of paper money. "Take it back, friend. You never heard me ask a man money for doin' a favor, least of all you. You're a damn' fool for makin' this try, but anything I got you're welcome to. I'll have everything set."

Llano spent a good twenty minutes deciding what to take in the way of guns. His final choice was the usual walnut-handled Colt .45 slung low in its holster at his thigh, another in a seldom-worn spring holster at his left armpit beneath his vest.

At ten o'clock he swung his three-team Barlow-Sanderson in behind the loading platform alongside Bob Morley's private office at the smelter. The cherry-red glow from the two high chimneys gave the four men who immediately came from the office enough light to work by. Llano had nothing to say beyond—"Make it fast, gents!"—and old Bob Morley, one of the four, didn't once open his mouth as he helped lug out the heavy, burlap-wrapped bars and hand them up to Llano to be stored in the boot, but twice he caught Llano's eye and each time he gave a sly wink.

It took seven minutes to load. Llano spent those seven minutes wondering which of these three Morley had picked as trustworthy men was the one who each time gave away the secret of these bullion shipments. The smelter had shipped only twice since the trouble started. Both times the stage had been stopped, its boots emptied, the driver and guard killed. Llano was sure of only one thing—the man who had betrayed Morley was working for someone higher up, someone with money and power living here in the obscurity of this wide-open boom town.

Wheeling the team down off the smelter grade and into the road, Llano took a last look back at the half-lit street. Even this late the walks at the town's center were packed. The four saloons hadn't once shut their doors during the eight months of this boom, nor had there been any break in the endless string of ore wagons coming down off the hill behind the town to the smelter.

The diggings had already turned out half a hundred fortunes. One of those fortunes should have been Llano's, for he had been the first in and had worked the stage concession from the beginning on the line to Butte. He had started with four Barlow-Sandersons and fourteen teams, barely enough equipment to handle the heavy traffic, and had made good money for six months. Then the raids had started, night raids on one out of every three stages that took the twisting road down out of the hills. In sixty days Llano had paid out $9,000 of his own money in damages to customers and for a week now had operated only one of his four coaches. Bob Morley had lost $14,000 in the same length of time, for Llano didn't insure bullion. If tonight's trip failed, Morley would have to let the smelter go and Llano would have to sell out to the highest bidder.

He found Pat's team and buckboard a dozen rods up the faintly marked fork that cut from the road directly below town. It took him twenty minutes to unhitch his three teams and lead them down into a grassy draw below the forks and stake them out for the night. Then, ignoring the stage and the load in its boot, he climbed to the seat of Pat Sewell's buckboard and drove back to town. He felt once for the Greener, found it on its rack under the seat.

Bob Morley's frame house was at the town's outskirts, 200 yards in from the smelter. There was hardly enough light tonight to distinguish a man's outline at fifty feet. For that reason Llano turned the team in at the hitch post in front of the house, making no attempt to hide his coming.

As he took the last step up onto the porch, a low, rich voice spoke from the shadows along the far railing: "It's you, Llano. I thought you'd gone."

The sound of that voice was something that always quickened Llano Ackers's interest, as it did now. It made him hurry his soft Texan's drawl a trifle as he answered: " 'Evenin', Mary. You're up late."

"I'm the reason, Llano," came a deeper-noted voice that Llano immediately identified as Ray Waldron's.

Llano was more irritated than surprised at finding the saloon owner here this evening. Each time he saw Ray Waldron call at the Morley house, each time he saw the man with Mary on the street, his irritation deepened until now he admitted that he hated Waldron for his own reasons. Llano had little use for an arrogant man; he had less use for one whose taste ran to varying shades of broadcloth, spotlessly clean white shirts, and fancy-stitched, beaded boots. Waldron was arrogant and his expensive outfits constantly reminded his acquaintances of a lacking in theirs.

Waldron owned the Paradise Club, and pointed to it with pride as being one of the town's most respectable businesses. It wasn't a wide-open saloon and didn't cater to the men who frequented Lode's other liquor parlors. It was located in a building on the town's single cross street, well away from the constantly thronged neighborhood of the stores. It had no swing doors, no painted sign to proclaim the nature of the establishment. Its single door was of plate glass, painted a dark green, unlighted.

Inside were three main rooms. Immediately inside the door was a luxurious red-and-gold furnished parlor where patrons could take their ease; back of that was the barroom, the bar of gold gilt, mirrors lining the walls, upholstered chairs spaced at proper intervals along the walls; the rear room was Waldron's gambling casino, the chief source of his income. Back there a man could play any gambling game known and for stakes as high as he wanted to name. No common miner from the diggings above town had ever seen the inside of the Paradise. Mine owners, speculators, business owners, and an assortment of splendidly dressed women were Waldron's patrons. It was a quiet, orderly, magnificent establishment.

Studying Waldron now, Llano found that he disliked even the man's looks. The short, thick-set body didn't fit the arrogant bearing; the smile Waldron's square face took on as he came up to Llano and thrust out a hand wasn't a cordial one.

"Congratulate me, Llano," Waldron said. "Mary has just said yes."

His words laid a coolness along Llano Ackers's nerves. Now that the news he'd been long expecting was put into words, Llano found it hard to say: "You're a lucky man, Waldron." He found it even harder to return the firm pressure of the man's grip.

Mary Morley came up and stood behind the man of her choice. "I'm lucky, too," she said, but her voice didn't carry conviction.

Llano stared at her intently, relying on the darkness to hide the sharpness of his scrutiny. Mary's oval face was set in a smile, but not the open smile of a girl happy in the presence of the man she loves. Llano understood several things in that brief moment, chief of which was the girl's reason in consenting to marry Waldron. Two months ago, when the trouble had begun, Bob Morley had needed money, needed it badly. There was no bank in Lode and the one at Butte had refused to make him a loan until he could guarantee safe delivery of bullion down out of the hills. Unable to do that, Morley had accepted Waldron's offer of money. The two raids on the bullion stages since then had wiped out any chances of repaying that loan immediately. Mary was taking this way out, and knowledge of what she was doing lessened Llano's respect for her father more than he cared to admit.

Llano was suddenly impatient to get away from here. "Go in and tell Bob I'm ready," he said to Mary, his voice sharper-edged than he liked. "Tell him we'll load out front." He watched her as she turned and went in at the door, noting that her step didn't have its customary lithe quickness. It bore the same lifeless quality of her expression of a moment ago.

"That's taking a chance, Llano," Ray Waldron said. "You might be seen."

"I'll risk it." Llano immediately understood that Waldron knew of their plans for the delivery of the bullion, grudgingly admitting that the man had a right to know. So he added as explanation: "I want to get downcañon as fast as I can and hit the Finger Rocks before they're expectin' the stage. That's where the trouble usually happens."

"I wonder who *they* are," Waldron said, reminding Llano of the mystery that lay behind the sudden recent raids of the unknown band of night riders.

The door opened and Bob Morley's stooped figure showed in the opening. "They're in the front room here, Llano," he said with a nervous laugh. "That pig iron we loaded onto the stage sure fooled the boys."

Llano stepped into the room's heavy darkness and from close to one side of him Morley said: "Here, on the floor." Llano leaped over and felt the stack and lifted one of the heavy bars of bullion and carried it out across the porch and down the steps.

Ray Waldron said—"Let me help."—and he and Morley followed Llano out to the buckboard, each carrying a blanket-wrapped bar of the precious yellow metal.

There were five bars of the gold alloy, worth five thousand apiece. When they were finally loaded, Bob Morley said: "I'll drag a couple bales of alfalfa from the shed out back if you say, Llano."

Llano shook his head. "Wouldn't look right. They're pretty well hidden."

He climbed to the seat, and was picking up the reins when Mary came to stand below him at the wheel hub. She reached up a hand, laid it lightly on his arm, and said softly: "Good luck, Llano."

Something balled up in Llano's throat and he couldn't answer. A lot depended on this trip to Butte tonight, more than any of them cared to admit. The thinly drawn temper within Llano abruptly cut loose. He said tersely—"I'll be all right."—and flicked the reins to set the team into motion.

II

His picture of Mary Morley's expression back there on the porch rode with Llano for almost five miles of that twisting, downcañon road. Once he had thought of the girl in the way Ray Waldron was thinking of her now, as being the one woman he'd ever ask to be his wife. All that was gone. That look had somehow robbed Mary of her beauty of even feature and deep brown eyes; it had made a mocking mask of the girl's face, and, remembering it, Llano Ackers felt something deeply inside him turn cold and hard at the knowledge of the sacrifice she was making.

The trail ran out across the cañon's first broad valley and out beneath the spreading branches of a huge cottonwood. He was too intent on his thoughts to catch even a hint of the shadow that suddenly swung down out of the low branches of that cottonwood as the buckboard ran beneath it. His first warning was the sudden lurch of the buckboard's springs taking up a man's falling weight. It was sheer instinct that made him drop the reins, stab his right hand toward holster, and turn on the seat.

He was too late. The man crouching behind was already swinging his six-gun in a merciless, down-chopping stroke. The weapon's barrel laid a vicious blow along Llano's temple. White sheets of light blinded him as he slumped backward off the seat. He tried to move, couldn't, and the last thing he heard as the team slowed to an abrupt stop was the sound of high-pitched laughter and a man's rasping voice calling: "Come and get it!"

When he was finally conscious of the throbbing pain in his head, Llano thought it was only seconds later, that the glare of light behind his closed lids was a fading out of the first blinding flash of the blow. He opened his eyes finally and saw that it was day.

He lay face up in the bed of the buckboard. His hand went to his swollen temple and came away sticky with half-dried blood. It took all his strength to sit up and brace himself against the sudden dizziness that sent his senses reeling. As soon as he could focus his eyes, he looked off to the left, saw Pat Sewell's team of browns grazing a few rods away across the valley floor, close to the fast-running stream that followed the cañon down out of the hills. Beyond, hugging the far slope of the valley's steep side, ran the light gravel grade of the road.

Llano crawled along the short length of the vehicle's bed, eased himself over the end gate, and tried to stand. When he found he couldn't, he went to his knees and crawled the thirty yards to the banks of the stream. The sharp coldness of the water steadied him, relieved his hot thirst. After five minutes he could stand without weaving on his feet.

The bullion was gone. He had his guns, Pat's Greener was slung under the seat, and no evidence remained of what had happened beyond the fresh scar made by a rowelled spur showing on one of the sideboards. Llano couldn't even think; there was nothing to think about. He pushed the team hard all the way to town. Bob Morley wasn't in his office at the smelter. No one answered his knock at the house's front door. He headed for the sheriff's office.

As he turned Pat's team in at the tie rail before the jail and saw the group on the walk that eyed him so soberly, he knew something was wrong. Harry Ross, the printer, was one of that group, alongside the jail office door. Stepping up onto the walk, Llano asked: "What's drawin' the crowd, Harry?"

Ross's bleakness of countenance didn't soften as he replied with surprising curtness: "You'll find out soon enough!"

Llano opened the jail office door and walked in, and broke his motion of closing the door before it was completed. Sheriff Bart Niven, standing in front of his desk alongside Spencer, his deputy, jerked the gun he held in his hand a bare inch, saying flatly: "Close it, Llano, close it! It's too late to run!" Then, as Llano slowly closed the door, the lawman nodded to Ray Waldron, standing to one side of the door. Waldron shrugged with a gesture of helplessness as Llano's glance swung around to regard him; he stepped in and lifted Llano's gun from its holster.

"He's wearin' one at his shoulder, too," Spencer said. "Get it, Ray." Waldron reluctantly relieved Llano of his second weapon.

Llano saw Mary and her father a second later as his eyes grew accustomed to the thick-walled room's semidarkness. Bob Morley was seated in a chair in a far corner of the room alongside the steel door that closed off the jail. The oldster's face was drawn and pale, and he looked at Llano with a hurt showing deeply in his blue eyes. Mary's look was like that, only that in her glance was the faint, bright quality of anger.

"Llano," she said abruptly, "tell them you didn't do it!"

Llano's curiosity was alive now, along with a deep, cold anger that made him look squarely at the sheriff and drawl: "You think I'd be fool enough to try and pack out of here with five bars of bullion?"

"That's a thought," Niven replied noncommittally. "Only I can't see why you came back."

"Easy, Sheriff," Ray Waldron said. "Llano's entitled to explain."

"There's nothin' to explain," Llano said, trying to keep his tones even. "All I remember is that whoever did it dropped out of the branches of that cottonwood in the upper valley. Caught me before I could move. He did this with his plow handle"— Llano raised his hand to the lump at his temple. "As I went out, I heard him call to someone. I even forget what he said." He waited, seeing instantly that his words brought no flicker of response in the sheriff's hard glance. All at once his anger let go. "You're a pack of fools if you think I framed this! I . . . "

"So the bullion's gone, eh? What about Pat Sewell?" Bart Niven was thin-faced, gray-mustached, and now his gaunt visage was granite-like in unyielding soberness. "What about that fight you and Pat had yesterday? What about his quittin' you last night?"

Llano jerked his head up, looked first at Mary,

and then at her father, trying to catch by their expression something that would explain the lawman's question. He could read nothing, and asked quickly: "What about Pat?"

In answer, the sheriff turned and picked a shiny bit of yellow metal off his cracked-varnish desk. It was a five-dollar gold piece with a hole through the center, the first money Llano had taken in on his new stage line, a lucky piece that never left his possession. Niven held it up between thumb and forefinger. "We found this in the ashes of Pat's fire. Pat fell onto his fire. It burned him pretty bad. Doc Moore says he wasn't dead when he fell. Maybe you can be glad at knowin' he was burned bad before he died. We aren't!"

In a split-second's time Llano knew the meaning behind the sheriff's words, that Pat was dead, that he was being accused of murdering his friend. It took him only that brief interval to close his fists and lunge forward. The sheriff made a futile stab at the gun he'd holstered a moment ago. His hand was brushing the weapon's handle when Llano's fist caught him high on one cheek bone. The force of the blow lifted the lawman's frail frame back across the desk. He crashed down hard onto his chair, the legs splintering and giving way, and he hit the floor on his shoulder blades and skidded two feet along the boards until his head hit solidly against the wall. His legs moved feebly, once, before his whole frame went loose in unconsciousness.

Llano was around the desk in one stride, stooping to snatch the six-gun from the sheriff's holster. It swung up and lined at Spencer before the deputy's hand had lifted his weapon from its holster. Ray Waldron, still holding Llano's guns in his hands, took care to stoop over and lay them on a chair alongside him.

"Mary?" Llano said. "I want to know what's happened. Who found Pat, where was he found, and how was he shot?"

Mary's voice was steady; there was a gladness in her eyes as she answered quickly: "He was found by an Irishman, a miner, on his way to work this morning. He . . . "

"What name?" Llano asked. He had leaned across and now carefully lifted Spencer's gun from its holster and laid it on the desk. "The Irishman, Mary? What was his name?"

"Maher," she told him. "Barney Maher. He's working with Findlay on his claim."

"Go on."

"Pat was shot from behind with a Forty-Five, the doctor says. He fell across his fire. I . . . I guess he was burned badly before he died. . . ." Mary's voice broke a little, then steadied. "Llano, before you go, I want you to know I believe you. I know you didn't do this. Dad and I will always remember how you tried to help us."

Llano had a brief moment of wonder at Mary's knowing that he meant to break his way out of here, to shoot if necessary. Then he said: "Bob, I want to hear you say that, too. I want to be sure."

Bob Morley's words came slow and haltingly. "I've tried for the last hour to talk Niven out o' makin' this play. That's why we're here, Llano. He was gettin' ready to round up a posse."

Llano smiled thinly as he regarded Ray Waldron. His dislike for the man was alive now; he took a grim pleasure in seeing the man flinch as his weapon swung around to line at him. "You, Waldron . . . !" The saloon owner gave a visible start of surprise. "You'll take over the smelter now? You close out on Morley?"

Ray Waldron shrugged, tried to look helpless, didn't quite manage it. "What else is there to do? A technicality, I'll admit, but necessary."

Llano queried: "Technicality?"

"It'll stay in the family," Waldron told him.

Llano had forgotten Mary's promise of last night. Remembering it now sobered him instantly. He picked up Spencer's gun, rammed it in his belt, and drawled: "Keep off the street for the next two minutes. I'm goin' to steal a horse and there may be trouble for anyone tryin' to stop me."

On the way across to the door he picked up his two weapons from the chair behind Waldron, put them in their holsters. There was a scattered crowd out front. As Llano appeared, the crowd broke in front of him and he was for the moment thankful that the jail walls and door were thick enough to have blanked out any sound of what had happened inside.

He walked to the hitch rail, took his pick of the four ponies tied there, and climbed into the saddle of a bay gelding. The stirrups were too short.

He was swinging out into the street when a shout came from down the walk: "Stop him! That's my horse!"

Llano bent low in the saddle as he drove in his spurs. A second later the throaty roar of a shot cut loose behind him and a bullet kicked up dust twenty feet farther along the street.

That single shot was the only one that followed Llano down the street. In another two seconds an angle between the false-fronted buildings hid him from the crowd at the jail. At the edge of town, the bay at a fast trot, he waved to the driver of an ore wagon and the man called out as he passed: "Nice mornin', Llano!"

Back from Bob Morley's house after a futile wait to hear from the sheriff's posse that was searching for Llano, Ray Waldron unlocked his office, entered it, and locked the door after him. His polished mahogany desk and swivel chair to match had been freighted into Lode from San Francisco along with the rest of the Paradise's furnishings, and now he took the chair, reached for a cigar, and lit it. As he leaned back, inhaling the richness of the pure Havana tobacco, a slow, satisfied smile widened the line of his thick lips. That smile stayed there until the knock sounded at his door.

He rose, crossed the room unhurriedly, and without opening the door called: "Who's there?"

A muffled voice answered—"Me."—and Waldron pushed back the bolt and swung the panel open.

Sheriff Burt Niven stepped in quickly, closing the door and bolting it. He turned to Waldron and said gruffly: "This isn't so good, Ray. Someone might see me."

"What of it?" came Waldron's crisp query. "We're tryin' to get that bullion back, aren't we?"

Niven's frown broke to a smile as he nodded. The smile was short-lived. "He's gone. We hung onto the sign as far as that bald rock two miles above. There's a hundred ways a man could take out of there."

"He's as good gone as dead," Waldron said. "Forget him."

The lawman shook his head slowly, deliberately. "I ain't so sure." His hand came up gingerly to touch the red mark of the bruise along his high cheek bone. "Any gent that'll make a play like he did back there at the jail don't forget easy. He may be back."

"It won't do him any good." Waldron took another long pull at the cigar. "The Wells Fargo man arrives tonight. Get that lawyer busy on that title for the equipment. By tonight I want clear title to everything Llano Ackers brought in here . . . teams, coaches, his lease on the station. I can't do my business any other way."

"How you goin' to guarantee Wells Fargo that their stages won't have the same trouble Llano's did?"

"Niven, a man without brains wouldn't have come as far as I have. Didn't you know that Llano was holdin' up his own stages? This was to be his last trip before he hightailed from the country, a rich man. He's gone now, and I'll personally make good any losses Wells Fargo has in makin' this run from Lode to Butte."

"Not bad," Niven conceded, his tight smile returning. "Not bad. Only I still say you've got to watch out for Llano. A couple weeks ago I saw him outdraw a gun-thrower from Wyomin' . . . the one that got that broken wrist and spent two nights in jail before we shipped him out. Llano was shaded on that draw but made his play and beat this jasper. He's got guts and he's fast . . . damned fast!"

Waldron laughed. "Guts, sure. But what good will they do him now? There's nothin' to prove on us. Tomorrow I leave for a trip to Denver. On the way out I head up to Gunshot Cañon and dig up the bullion and put it in my trunk. At Denver I climb onto the Union Pacific. That friend of mine in Saint Louis will be satisfied with a quarter split on the bullion and take it off our hands. I'll be back in ten days with your money and Spencer's. We can forget about Llano."

Niven rubbed his hands together, a greedy look in his eyes. "Then I can tell this law job to go to hell. This winds it up."

"And throw over the nicest set-up any two men ever had?" Waldron shook his head. "Unh-uh, Bart. You play along with me and we'll try another thing or two. Remember, I own the smelter now. There's a few big mines that aren't usin' the smelter, one that may build one of its own. Between the two of us we ought to be able to show them how they'll make money usin' ours."

"How?"

Waldron shrugged, lifted his brows. "Who knows? Maybe their ore wagons will have bad luck with broke axles. Maybe it'll be hard to get drivers when a few have had their hats shot off."

"I get it." Niven paused to consider. "As you say, Ray, make it worth my while and I'll wear this badge until the nickel comes off."

Waldron's glance went cold for a fleeting instant. "Was there ever a time when I didn't make it worth your while?"

Niven's look narrowed. He came over to stand by the desk, putting his two clenched fists on it, leaning toward Waldron as he said: "We don't need Spencer. His share's a tenth and he didn't earn it. And I'm not so sure about him when he drinks. He talks."

"Then get rid of him."

"For his share?" The lawman stared down at Waldron intently.

Ray Waldron had an understanding of understrappers acquired from long experience. They were good until they put too much value on their services. Bart Niven had had a fifth share of the proceeds from the two previous raids on Llano Ackers's stages; his wanting Spencer's tenth in addition to his own was all the evidence Ray Waldron now needed to convince him that Niven was going the way of all understrappers. Yet he gave no hint of what he knew as he answered easily: "Sure, I'll handle Spencer before I leave tomorrow and you can have his tenth. That bullion will be worth thirty thousand to my friend in Saint Louis. That's three thousand more for you. Play along with me, Bart, and we'll clean up more than these mine owners before we pull out of this country."

After Niven left, Waldron sat a long while in his chair, studying a pencil he turned idly in his fingers. When he finally tossed the pencil onto his desk, he had decided on the man who would be Lode's new sheriff.

He was unusually affable that night as he ate his evening meal with Mary Morley and her father. After they left the table, Mary going to the kitchen to do the dishes, Bob Morley reluctantly brought up the thing that had been on his mind all day. He opened a drawer of the china cabinet and took out a piece of paper, a pen, and a bottle of ink. Coming back to take the chair alongside the one where Waldron sat, he said: "Here's the title, Ray. I'll sign it over to you."

Waldron held up a protesting hand. "Not now, Bob. This can be taken care of anytime. As I said this morning, it's a pure technicality."

"It's an obligation," Morley insisted, the worry showing in his eyes, in the deep wrinkles of his high forehead. "Your loan was for twenty thousand. The smelter cost me a little over thirty to build. We'll draw up a new title, giving me a third interest in the business. I'll stay on as superintendent if you want." He uncorked the ink bottle, dipped the pen in it, and held it out to the saloon owner.

Waldron reached out and took the pen with a show of reluctance. "I don't want to do this, Bob. But if you'll feel better havin' it this way . . . "

His words broke off as glass crashed inward at the window behind him. His thick-set frame went rigid and he turned in his chair in time to see a hand holding a six-gun reach through the broken pane and thrust aside the curtain.

Abruptly Llano Ackers's drawling voice spoke out: "I'll take that title, Waldron. Hand it across!"

"Llano!" Bob Morley's face was pale and drawn. "Llano, this is a personal affair. Keep out of it!"

"I'll still take that title."

Ray Waldron's left side was toward the window. As Llano spoke, the saloon owner's right hand slowly went in under his coat and raised toward the shoulder holster he always wore at his left armpit.

Suddenly Llano's thumb drew back the hammer of his weapon. The gun exploded in a blasting concussion that made the flame of the lamp flicker. Waldron groaned and let his right arm fall, his left hand crossing to clench the fiery burn Llano's bullet had laid along his upper arm. His rugged face drained of all color, and he picked up the title and hurriedly handed it across. Llano's other hand showed in the window a moment as he reached in to take the folded sheet of paper. Then both hand and gun drew back out of sight.

Bob Morley stood there, fascinated a brief moment before he ran for the front door. He threw it open, called loudly—"Llano!"—but had his only answer in the abrupt hoof drum of a running pony as it went fast down the road and out of town.

Mary was standing in the kitchen doorway as her father came back in the door. He looked at her, saw with surprise that she was smiling. "That was Llano, wasn't it?" she asked.

Ray Waldron muttered irritably: "There's a gun in the kitchen you might have used."

She smiled, and answered: "That wouldn't have been fair, Ray."

He was more worried than he cared to admit even to himself as he walked back to the Paradise. He could have a new title drawn up and recorded, but that would take time. The Paradise rooms were filling and it took him ten minutes to work his way back to his office, stopping several times on the way to talk to a few of his wealthier patrons.

Once in his office he pulled his coat off, rolled up his shirt sleeves, and wrapped a clean handkerchief about the shallow, bloody flesh wound on his arm. Now was no time to call in Doc Moore. The medico would be too curious.

The cigar clenched between his teeth was burned down to a bare inch when Bart Niven knocked at the door and ushered in a man he introduced as: "Mister Baker of Wells Fargo, Ray. He stopped me to ask the way to your place, so I brought him along myself."

The sheriff left, and, as the door closed behind him, Baker said abruptly: "I'll make this as brief as possible, Waldron. I learned an hour ago that you today purchased the Ackers Stage Lines. I called on your lawyer, found your title clear and in order. But we aren't in the market for this run at the present time. So we're holding off."

"Because of the trouble we've been having?" Waldron said. Catching Baker's answering nod, he went on easily: "You know, of course, that Llano Ackers was robbing his own outfits, that . . . "

Baker's jaw muscles tightened. "I know no such thing," he cut in. "But I do know Llano Ackers, met him down in Texas five years ago where he got his start . . . and his name. Do you happen to know, Waldron, how he got that name?"

The saloon owner shook his head, sensing at once that he'd said the wrong thing.

"Llano was the only man down there who'd take a stage across that neck of the Staked Plains . . . the Llano Estacado . . . between Cherokee and Antelope. The Comanches still take a scalp now and then down there. Llano Ackers got his name fightin' Comanches at damned slim pay. He's as honest as any man I know." Baker shook his head. "You're makin' a wrong guess, Waldron. Llano Ackers wasn't responsible for this trouble. We won't buy you out until you find out who is responsible."

Waldron was for the first time in his life speechless, caught without one idea that would carry his point, clinch this bargain he'd been framing for months. Baker, thinking the saloon owner's silence came from embarrassment at having wrongly accused a man, said: "I'll wish you good night. Let my Denver office know when this trouble clears up." He turned without further ceremony and left the office.

III

Barney Maher's tent was the fourth in line of the double row that flanked the line of the high bench above Lode, close to the diggings. Barney was one of the less important citizens of this settlement some-one had dubbed Little Ireland. It was a weekday and the last lantern in the tents winked out shortly after Llano tied his stolen bay gelding in a thicket of cedar after making the climb from Morley's house, an hour after dark.

He waited there twenty minutes longer, knowing that he was giving himself all the time necessary; these Irishmen put in a hard day's work and were quick, heavy sleepers. As he started down the slope, walking carefully, soundlessly, his right hand reached into the pocket of his Levi's and touched the folded sheet of paper. Remembering how Ray Waldron's hand had shaken as he had handed the smelter title across brought a thin smile to Llano's lips, an amused look to his gray eyes.

He came down directly behind Barney Maher's

tent and was careful as he stepped between the guy ropes. As his right hand palmed the heavy Colt .45 from its holster at his thigh, his left went out to lift up the canvas drop. He reached in and felt the side bar of Barney's cot at the precise instant the Irishman's bulk stirred restlessly and he jerked awake. Llano stepped into the tent, rammed his weapon into Barney's ribs, and drawled softly: "Quiet, Barney."

Maher's voice grated in a harsh whisper: "Bud, what be yer . . . ?"

"Outside," Llano said softly, reaching down to lift the drop alongside him. He could make out Maher's shape in the darkness now. "Get down and crawl, Barney. And careful. I'm nervous with a hog-leg."

Three minutes later Barney stood with half-raised hands alongside the bay at the cedar thicket up the hill above the tents. Llano, two paces away, was rolling a cigarette. When he finished, he offered Barney the makings. "Smoke?"

Now that Llano's gun was holstered, the man's nerve was coming back. "Smoke be damned!" he flared. "Ye'll tell me what ye're about!"

"About this mornin', Barney. About findin' Pat."

"And what about thot?"

"You work at Findlay's diggings. The spot where you found Pat this mornin' isn't on the way from here to Findlay's. Were you out for an early mornin' walk, Barney?"

"As if 'twas any o' yer damn' business! I'll have me partners beatin' the bush for the likes of ye in another minute."

Llano's reach for his six-gun was a deceptively lazy gesture. But it swung up so fast that Barney didn't have quite the time to get his hands down. "I could lick you one-handed, Barney, but I haven't the time. Tell me how you happened to find Pat this mornin' or I'll let the wind out of your guts with all five of these slugs." As he finished, he cocked the gun, the hammer click sounding audibly in the stillness.

Barney Maher's Irish blood was his only claim to courage. Just now his upraised hands trembled visibly. "Be swingin' that off me, Llano," he said, his tone frantic. "'Twas a shame about Pat. And 'twill do me heart good to name ye the man that paid me fifty dollars to go find him. Niven, it was. Him that wears the sheriff's star. And I say he's no damned good!"

Llano spent a good ten seconds letting this unexpected news settle in his mind. In his eight months' stay in Lode he'd developed a healthy dislike for the lawman. Niven was a close-mouthed, sour, surly individual, yet here was the first proof Llano had ever had of the lawman's being dishonest. This afternoon he'd thought back over every detail of last night's happenings and decided that Ray Waldron was the only man aside from himself, Mary, and Bob Morley who had known that the bullion was being taken out in Pat Sewell's buckboard. Now, to have this proof against Bart Niven link him with Waldron took Llano a little closer to discovering who had murdered Pat Sewell.

"Can you ride a horse, Barney?" he asked the Irishman. "Can you ride from here down to Butte in time to be on the mornin' stage for Pueblo?"

"Be tellin' me why I should give up me job with Findlay?"

"Because by mornin' the sheriff will know you've talked. If I was him, I'd frame Pat's murder on you."

Barney Maher's jaw slacked open, then snapped shut. He swallowed with difficulty, saying hoarsely: "Ye'd frame me with that?"

"Not me, but Niven. You can take your choice, Barney. Either come down to the livery barn with me and steal a horse and leave, or take your chances of outfightin' your own mob. Pat knew half the men in this camp. They liked him. They'll hang the man that shot him."

Barney let out his breath in a gusty sigh. "And I was makin' me good wages, too," he said. There wasn't any more fight in him. He walked down the steep trail to the town, never once looking back at Llano, who rode a few feet behind him. Llano helped Barney let down the bars at the back of the feed barn corral, helped him cinch tight a saddle they found on a rack inside the broad maw of the barn's open back door.

As the Irishman swung up into the saddle, Llano said: "They still hang a man for stealin' a horse in this country, Barney. That makes you guilty on two counts. You'd better hurry."

Barney hurried, circling the street until he reached the downgrade of the road well beyond town. Llano's bay was a fast horse but the animal had a hard time keeping Barney in sight the three miles Llano rode to make sure his bluff had carried.

Llano rode back to Lode, climbed his bay well up onto the bench where sprawled the tents of Little Ireland, then tied the animal well back in the cedars before he took the path downward that led to the town's main street. He pulled his Stetson low over his eyes, crossing the main thoroughfare to take the unlighted side street and walk down it to a point opposite the Paradise. He paused there, considering how he could get inside the place and back to Ray Waldron's office without being discovered, for he had made up his mind to see Waldron tonight, to get the truth out of him.

He had smoked a cigarette and had flicked it out onto the street, was about to cross to the Paradise's front door and trust to luck, when that door opened and the light from inside was thrown strongly on the face of a man who stepped out. Llano knew that face, remembered it, and immediately a curiosity as to the reasons for this man's presence here took a hold on him.

He had known Abner Baker down in Texas well enough to know that Baker wasn't the kind to frequent a place like the Paradise, nor the kind to have dealings with a man like Ray Waldron. He quickly decided that his own business with Waldron could wait, and crossed over and followed Baker along the walk almost to the corner of the main street before he called out: "Baker!"

The Wells Fargo man stopped, turned, his hand sliding in at his waist beneath his coat. But when the shadowy figure behind announced—"It's me, Llano Ackers."—Baker's hand came empty from inside his coat and his long face took on a pleased smile and he exploded: "I'll be damned!"

They shook hands, and Baker's face sobered abruptly. "What's this I hear about your bein' in trouble?"

"Can you find a place where we can talk alone?"

Baker said: "I'm at the Mountain House, Room Fourteen. Meet me there in five minutes."

Llano used the hotel's back stairs, coming in

along the alley. His soft knock on the door of Room
Fourteen was immediately answered and he
stepped inside without being seen.

Baker took off his coat, threw it on the bed, and
said: "I'm glad I saw you. What's Waldron got up
his sleeve?"

Llano shrugged. "You tell me."

"He's offered to sell Wells Fargo your stage line
for twenty thousand, cash. I came here to buy it, but
things didn't smell so good."

For a moment Llano was speechless, hearing this
news for the first time. He had known, of course,
that his small business would immediately be sold
by the sheriff as an outlaw's property. But the suddenness of the thing, the fact that Waldron was the
buyer and had taken less than a day to make his
purchase, was what struck him. That, and Baker's
being here by prearrangement to buy the stage line
from Waldron, were the final proofs that convinced
Llano of the saloon owner's guilt.

He told Baker as much as he knew, beginning
with the first robbery of one of his stages two
months ago, the killing of both driver and guard,
and the disappearance of a mine payroll. He told of
his difficulty in getting men to work for him until
Pat Sewell was the only one loyal enough to stick
with him, and finally of his argument with Pat yesterday afternoon.

"About last night," Baker said. "Waldron knew
how you were to take the gold out?"

Llano supplied all the details.

Baker sat without speaking a long moment; finally his glance narrowed shrewdly and he said:
"Waldron couldn't have cleared his title to your out-

fit if he hadn't had the sheriff's help. And you know definitely that Niven paid that Irishman to find Sewell. That lines him up pretty well alongside Waldron all the way through."

"But for a sheriff to . . . " Llano abruptly checked his words as he heard the sound of upraised voices coming from in front of the nearest saloon, two doors below the hotel.

A man down there suddenly called in a whiskey-thickened voice: "Clear out o' my way or damn' if I won't whip in your thick skull, Spencer!"

Then a voice Llano recognized as Deputy Sheriff Milo Spencer's shouted stridently: "Someone give me a hand with this gent! He's drunk and he might . . . " Other voices, raised in alarm, muted the deputy's words. But something in the high-pitched quality of Spencer's voice fanned alive a spark of memory within Llano.

Abruptly he smashed one fist into his other open palm, drawling: "Baker, I've got something! The gent that gunwhipped me under that cottonwood last night was the sheriff's deputy."

"That's a guess, Llano," Baker said. "You told me you didn't recognize the voice."

"Listen!" Llano said. Once more Spencer's voice sounded above the others, boots scuffled along the plank walk below the window, and suddenly the commotion ceased. "That was Spencer arrestin' a drunk. He yelled a minute ago, and that voice was the same one I heard last night. I'm sure of it, Baker."

"Then there's at least three of them in on it. With the law on Waldron's side, you'll have a poor chance of provin' anything."

Llano leaned forward in his chair, eyeing his friend soberly. "Spencer and at least one other man stopped me last night. It's not like Bart Niven to trust a gold shipment worth thirty thousand dollars to a deputy who might jump the country with it. I'll lay my bet that Niven was the one with Spencer last night."

"And if he was?" Baker queried.

"They both knew where the bullion was hidden. Baker, Niven's goin' to double-cross his deputy tonight."

"I don't get it, Llano."

"Get a sheet of paper and a pencil and write what I tell you," Llano said.

Milo Spencer had his hands full with the drunk he arrested at the saloon below the hotel. The man hadn't had enough whiskey to loosen his muscles, and he fought all the way to the jail. When he was finally locked in his cell, Spencer knew he'd been working. He went into the jail office, turned down the lamp, and rolled a cigarette, glad to rest, tilted back in the sheriff's chair, his feet on the desk. He'd have to wait here now until Bart Niven came back.

He'd had only an hour's sleep last night; it was already an hour past the time he usually turned in, and he was sleepy and comfortable. He threw the cigarette into the cuspidor alongside the desk, wanting to make sure it wouldn't fall out of his hand and burn a hole in his shirt, and then he let his chin sag comfortably onto his chest. He was asleep in two minutes.

Llano found him that way. The street door was ajar; the hinges didn't squeak as he pushed it open, and the wide planks of the floor were solid enough so that no sound gave away his step as he crossed the room and laid Baker's printed note in front of the sleeping deputy, fully in the glare of the lamp.

Outside, from across the street, Llano threw the broken half of a worn mule's shoe straight through the front jail window. He had stepped into the sheltering darkness of an alleyway between two buildings even before the glass across the way shattered loudly and fell to the walk.

The six-inch length of iron came through the window and hit Spencer a glancing blow on the thigh. It jerked him into instant wakefulness and his boots hit the floor with a thud as he lunged up out of his chair with hand lancing toward his holstered six-gun. Standing there with the weapon at his hip, staring stupidly at the broken window, he made a figure so ridiculous that he realized it and finally holstered his .45 and growled: "Why can't they let a man alone?"

Then he saw the sheet of paper on the desk. His scalp tingled as he read the poorly printed words: YOU AND WALDRON WATCH NIVEN.

At that precise instant Spencer recognized Bart Niven's boot tread on the plank walk outside. Frantic in his haste, he crumpled the paper and dropped it down the lamp chimney. The flame went ragged, smoked, but finally the paper caught and burned to an ash.

Niven came in, closed the door, and only then saw the glass shards scattered along the floor. He looked at Spencer, and the deputy said: "I got one of 'em locked in that back cell. His friends is outside."

"One what?"

"Drunk. They cut loose a half hour ago at the Bull's Head. Where were you?"

The truth of the matter was that Niven had gone from the Paradise to pay a call on a lady. So now he growled—"Where I was is none o' your business!"—and fanned into flame the spark of suspicion the scrap of paper had a moment ago raised in Spencer's mind.

The deputy said—"I'll clean up this mess in the mornin'."—and went out the door, taking care to keep his eye on the sheriff and not expose his back. He looked back over his shoulder all the way along the shadowed, awninged walk until he came to the side street and turned into it and headed for the Paradise.

Waldron's thin-drawn temper was plainly evident as Spencer came into the office. The saloon owner's arm was hurting from the crease of Llano's bullet; it hung in a cumbersome sling Waldron had made by tying two handkerchiefs together.

His fleshy, square face was set in a hard frown, and, as Spencer closed the door, he snapped out: "I told you never to come here!"

"Boss, I had to," Spencer said, holding up a hand to check the saloon owner's protest. "Listen, and see if I didn't." And he told Waldron of the note, what it had said, how it had been delivered while he was asleep.

Waldron's frown slacked off and his two cold, blue eyes became narrow-lidded. "Who wrote it?"

"It was printed."

Waldron was silent a moment. At length his clenched fist banged the desktop. "Someone's workin' with Niven. You know what this means, Spencer?"

The deputy shook his head, a little awed by the

magnificence of the room, the confidential tone Waldron was using with him.

"Niven spoke about gettin' rid of you this mornin'," Waldron went on, seeing that his words instantly brought a tide of color to Spencer's face. "I talked him out of it. Now it looks like he's out to hog all that bullion. Spencer, can I trust you?"

"I'll go back there now and blow his face in."

Waldron was a shrewd judge of a man. He was keen enough to be sure now that Milo Spencer meant what he said, that he could trust the man with anything. "That's the wrong way to do it, Spencer. The bullion comes first. The jasper that left that warning on your desk is probably the one Niven wanted to hire to bushwhack you and me. Maybe he's a friend of ours and turned Niven down. Tonight you're to take a pack horse and ride up Gunshot. Dig up the bullion and bring it here and we'll put it through the back window, then you and me are goin' to pay our call on Niven! Tomorrow you'll be Lode's sheriff!"

"He's mine, boss," Spencer breathed, hot hate showing in his glance. "I've thought for a long time he'd someday do this. I want to see a slug from my cutter spill his brains out of that thick skull!"

"He's yours, all right," said Waldron with an inscrutable smile, "after you've made that ride down Gunshot. I'll give you two hours."

When Spencer came out of the Paradise, Llano was hidden well in the shadow of a building across the street. He followed the deputy to the feed barn, was even close enough to the doors to hear Spencer say to the hostler inside: "Throw my hull on my roan, Tip, and put a pack saddle on one of your lugheads. And make it fast."

Llano read his own meaning into the deputy's words and walked the nearest way to the bench trail and climbed it to where he had tied his stolen bay gelding. Circling above the town and then sloping down into the cañon road, he knew he had to make a guess as to where Spencer was riding tonight. He kept the bay at a run, knowing that Spencer was in a hurry; he covered the five up-and-down miles to the cottonwood that overhung the trail in little more than half an hour.

He made his guess from there, crossing the broad floor of the valley and working back toward Lode. Half a mile back along the gradual upgrade brought him to the narrow mouth of Gunshot Cañon, an off-shoot of this broad valley.

He waited there, and was well hidden in a growth of scrub oak when the hoof slur of Spencer's fast-trotting horses echoed out from this near side of the valley. He clamped a hand over the bay's nostrils in time to keep the animal from nickering a warning and giving away his presence. He was close enough to the twisting narrow entrance of Gunshot to make out Spencer's shadowy form as he rode past.

IV

Many times on the way down the road to Butte, Llano had studied the sloping walls of the cañon as it broadened to make these wide valleys. Its rim towered too high to leave a way out at the head of these narrow box cañons that were offshoots of the larger one. So now he felt fairly certain that Milo Spencer would have to ride back this way in leaving Gunshot.

Spencer did ride out of the mouth of that narrow defile twenty minutes later. Llano, less than twenty feet to one side of the opening, let go his grip on the bay's nostrils when he saw the bulk on the back of the pack horse the deputy was leading.

His bay snorted, and, as Spencer's bulk went rigid in the saddle, Llano commanded: "Reach, Milo!"

Spencer was a bull-headed man. He jerked on the reins, rammed his spurs into the roan's flanks. But the animal had taken only one stride when Llano's .45 bucked. Spencer's hat whirled from his head and fell to the sandy ground. No man but a fool would have taken chances against a gun in the hands of a man who could throw a bullet with the accuracy Llano had shown. Spencer was no fool. He reined the roan to a standstill and raised his hands.

"That's more like it," Llano drawled, stepping in close and reaching up to relieve the deputy of his single holstered six-gun. "You were takin' the bullion back to Waldron, weren't you, Milo?"

"You'll play hell findin' out," Spencer growled.

Llano stepped back alongside the pack horse, pulled aside one corner of the dirt-smeared blankets to catch the reflected glint of starlight from one of the shiny bars of bullion before he said: "Climb down, friend."

Spencer knew what was coming, yet was powerless to avoid it. Years ago Llano had learned the timing and sureness of a blow struck with a six-gun barrel that can knock a man into unconsciousness without crushing his skull. He had never hit a man from behind and didn't do it now. He drew his left-hand Colt, feinted a blow with it. Spencer dodged, and the downstriking gun in Llano's right fist caught the deputy as surely as though he'd been standing motionlessly. His knees buckled and he went down.

Forty minutes later Llano was knocking at the door of Bob Morley's frame house at the outskirts of Lode. He had to wait for a good ten seconds before a lamp's light flickered on inside. The door opened and Bob Morley stood there with the lamp in his hand, his jaw slacking open when he saw Llano with Spencer's bulk thrown across his shoulder.

"Get your light away from the door," Llano said quickly, stepping inside.

He eased Spencer's limp frame to the floor as Morley swung the door shut. In the dim glow of the lamp Llano looked across the room and saw Mary standing in the doorway to her bedroom, a quilted robe wrapped tightly about her slender body, a rifle held in her two hands. Sight of the rifle brought a smile to Llano's lean face. "You aren't takin' any chances with me, are you?"

Bob Morley said: "See here, Llano! You know what you're doin', but I don't. First you bust in a window and run off with the deed to the smelter, now you lug a dead man in here." The oldster's glance fell to the figure on the floor. His breath came in a quick gasp. "Goddlemighty, it's Spencer!"

Llano stepped over to lean down and lift the deputy's frame from the floor and ease it into a rocker. He turned to Mary. "We'll need a bucket of water to bring him to. Between us, we have to make him talk." The girl and her father exchanged surprised glances, but Mary went to the kitchen and returned with a pail of water.

A minute later, Spencer caught his breath, gasped, and his eyes fluttered open after Llano threw the first dipperful of water squarely into his face. His eyes at first stared vacantly around him, then he saw Llano and his glance took on a look of mingled hate and stubbornness.

Llano said quietly: "Bob, I caught Spencer comin' out of Gunshot Cañon with your bullion laced to the back of a pack horse. Earlier tonight, Spencer was in the Paradise for a long talk with Ray Waldron. What's his game?"

"The bullion," old Bob Morley breathed. His wide-open and staring brown eyes quickly became narrow-lidded in shrewdness. Suddenly he said: "Ray Waldron was the only one besides us that knew how that bullion was bein' shipped last night."

Llano was looking at Spencer. "Milo, an hour ago I had a talk with Barney Maher. He told me . . . "

Spencer all at once lunged up out of his chair, his arms swinging wildly, one of his fists striking Llano on the shoulder. But the lean Texan's one striking blow caught the deputy fully in the mouth, knocked him back down into the chair with such force that one of the black rungs gave way with a brittle crack. Spencer raised a hand and wiped it across his bloody lips, glaring up defiantly.

Llano went on: "Barney talked, told me how you paid him fifty dollars to take a walk this mornin' and find Pat's body."

"That's a lie!" Spencer flared, sitting erect in the chair, gripping the arms with hands white-knuckled. "Niven took care of that. I didn't have a thing to do with it." All at once he eased back in the chair, muttering: "So it was Barney that left the note, him that Niven tried to hire for the bushwhack."

Llano said: "Maybe you'd like to tell us about it, Milo. We might go easier on you later."

For a brief moment he didn't know how well his frameup had carried. But as Spencer's glance took on a look of cunning, reading the inner workings of the man's mind as he thought of Bart Niven, Llano knew he had won. In another moment the deputy was saying: "I'll talk. Damned if I'll take a rawhidin' and let those two off! It was Niven that shot Pat Sewell, him and me that took care of you down the cañon last night, and buried the bullion up at Gunshot. Waldron hired us, me for a tenth share, Niven for a fifth."

"How about the other times?" Llano queried. "How much has Waldron paid you for workin' for him in the last three months?"

Abruptly came the deputy's realization that he had talked too much. A mirthless smile now set across his rugged visage. "You'd like to know, wouldn't you?"

Llano straightened, looked across at Bob Morley. The smelter owner's eyes were wide in obvious amazement. He was held speechless at what he had heard. Finally Llano said: "We'll have to tie him up until he can tell his story to a judge."

Ten minutes later Mary Morley's two lengths of clothesline bound Milo Spencer so tightly he couldn't move. At his first loud oath, Llano had tied a tight gag about his mouth. Spencer's face was now flushed with crimson deepened by his futile struggles against the stout rope.

Llano said—"Watch him until I get back."—and went to the door and opened it.

"Llano! Wait!" Mary crossed the room and stood in front of him, her glance coming up to meet his. "I want you to know I'm sorry for what I did last night. But . . . it seemed like the only way out."

It may have been that this moment was the first in which Bob Morley fully understood the sacrifice his daughter had made in promising to marry Ray Waldron. For as her words ended, he spoke from across the room, beginning—"I've been ten kinds of a fool . . ."—and abruptly checked what he'd meant to say in the realization that neither Mary nor Llano had heard him.

The girl's glance as she looked up at Llano was filled with a tenderness old Morley had never before seen there. Llano's gray eyes mirrored something of the girl's look; they were no longer slate-hard and inscrutable.

Mary said quietly: "You're going to the Paradise, aren't you, Llano?"

He nodded, and that gesture brought a return of the granite-like quality to his eyes.

"Will you be careful, Llano . . . for me?" she said softly.

The thing that was in her eyes, the tenderness and the promise that lay behind her words, were things Llano Ackers knew he must ignore. This girl now, as never before, was infinitely desirable. Abruptly he knew that another moment with her would soften him beyond doing the task he'd set himself.

That was his reason for turning abruptly and going out the door and closing it behind him. All the way into town, until he turned into the side street toward the Paradise, Mary's image was a clear picture before him. Then, as he opened the saloon's plate-glass door, he put all thoughts of her aside.

The Paradise was crowded. He made his way across the parlor inside the door, catching the surprised stares of several men who knew him, of ladies whose glances raised in surprised query at seeing his outfit of dusty Levi's, faded Stetson, and jingling spurs in these luxurious surroundings. He went through the wide doors into the barroom, and came face to face with Bart Niven.

At sight of him, the lawman stepped with feet spread a little, hands at his sides, his fingers clawing slowly toward his guns. Llano took one step that put his back to the near wall and drawled: "Start it when you like, Bart."

A hush had settled across these two rooms as people caught a hint of the violence that was forming. The far door to the gambling room opened and Ray Waldron stepped through, not seeing immediately what was happening, but breaking his choppy stride when his glance finally crossed the room and settled first on Bart Niven, then Llano.

Waldron spoke sharply: "Ed, get him!" The bartender took a step along the bar and reached a hand in under his counter.

Llano understood the apron's gesture. No one was expecting the flashing move of his right hand that smoothly palmed the Colt out of its holster. His weapon swung out of its line with Niven and blasted its throaty roar once. The barkeep's shirt at the base of his neck split open and the mirror behind him suddenly spider-webbed as the bullet crashed into it. He straightened fast and threw up his hands, his shotgun under the bar forgotten.

The welling echo of that shot brought two sober-faced men in from the gambling room at Waldron's back. One's hand had already brushed aside his coat from holster. But staring across into the blunt snout of Llano's gun he took his hand carefully away.

From a far corner of the room a woman's scream suddenly wiped out the awed hush that had followed the gun's explosion. Llano said: "No one'll get hurt if they leave quietly."

It took less than thirty seconds for the room to empty, the front door in the parlor at Llano's back squeaking continually on its poorly oiled hinges. When there was quiet out there, when Llano faced

Bart Niven and Waldron's two hired gunhands, he said softly: "Now who's drawin' cards in this hand?"

Llano waited for the thing that didn't happen, the first move of one of them for a gun. A sudden impatience took its hold on him. "I can't shoot a man who hasn't the guts to draw!" Even that brought no response.

A fragile, thin-backed chair stood alongside Llano. A thought made him pick it up with his left hand and throw it in a long arc that sent it crashing across the bar and into the expensive mirror behind.

Niven growled: "Go ahead. Wreck the place and have your fun! You won't get out alive!"

Llano took two steps that got him alongside the near end of the cherry-wood bar. "That's an idea, Bart." His gun leveled, he lifted one foot and put it against the inside corner of the long bar and pushed. The counter toppled outward, overbalanced, and fell slowly and with a sound of splitting wood, breaking glass.

"Still no takers," Waldron said. But Llano saw that his right arm was bent at the elbow, that his face was drawn and white, and that he was waiting for his chance. The apron, realizing what was shaping up, sidled across to the gaming-room door and disappeared through it.

Llano caught the glint of reflected light from the barrel of his six-gun. That flash of color brought his attention up to the four-foot-wide crystal chandelier hanging at the center of the ceiling. It was suspended by a gilt chain. Llano was enjoying this destruction, knowing that every broken piece of these gaudy furnishings was the needed pinprick to gall

Ray Waldron into an open fight. So now he jerked up the barrel of his six-gun and thumbed a shot upward. The middle link of the chandelier chain snapped in two.

The outer rim of the heavy falling ring of kerosene lamps caught Bart Niven on the shoulder, knocked him down. As he fell, he reached for his gun, arched it up, and fired a shot at Llano that went wild.

When Llano's gun swung around to cover the sheriff, Ray Waldron moved his hand up to his shoulder holster. The two men behind him lunged out of line, hands slamming toward their weapons.

Llano had barely time to line his gun before the sheriff's blasted out a second time directly at him. The slam of the bullet that took him low on one thigh spoiled his aim for the fraction of a second. Then his six-gun bucked in his hand and Bart Niven's head jerked inhumanly from the crush of the lead slug and a blue hole centered his temple as he fell to the floor.

The fifteen lamps of the chandelier burst as they hit the floor, throwing flaming kerosene in a rough six-foot circle across the fine carpeting. Against this sudden blaze, the only light in the room now, Llano Ackers had a quick glimpse of three guns flashing out of holsters, lining at him. He threw his long frame in behind the overturned bar in time to feel the bullet-whip of Waldron's first shot along his right arm. Two more explosions cut loose to prolong that of Waldron's gun.

On the heel of that deafening triple concussion, Llano raised his head and six-gun above the protection of the thick cherry-wood counter. His one snap shot knocked the man in front of Waldron back into the saloon owner. Waldron pushed his gunman aside, knocking him to the floor, and was swinging his .45 into line as Llano lowered his head again.

The acrid odor of scorched wool filled the air a moment later as the rug started burning. The flickering light of the flames threw deceiving shadows along the far wall as Llano waited for the next shot, listening carefully into the sudden stillness. Abruptly a hint of sound shuttled back along the planks of the bar and with it he was rolling toward the back wall, seeing the shape of Waldron's second gunman halfway the length of the bar, stepping toward him.

The man fired two quick shots at Llano's smoke-shrouded shape. One of the bullets chipped a floor plank at his left elbow. The second plowed a two-inch gash along the bunched cap muscle at his right shoulder. He stopped rolling when he lay against the wall and lifted his six-gun and aimed at the center of that killer's high shadow.

His gun's pounding explosion seemed to drive back that shadow. It stumbled awkwardly, the smoke thinned for an instant, and Llano saw the man go down, his clawed hands ripping open his shirt at his stomach.

A glance of powder flame showed in a far corner, the bullet of that shot fanning the air in front of Llano's face. Waldron was over there, momentarily hidden by the smoke and the flickering light of the mounting flames and smoke. Llano came to his knees and pushed against the wall, bracing himself against the numbness of his wounded leg, choking against the bite of the smoke-fogged air at his lungs. Ray Waldron was the only man that faced him now.

After that single answering shot of Waldron's, a quarter-minute silence dragged out interminably. Llano didn't move, staring across the flaming circle of rug and through the smoke, trying to see Waldron. Suddenly a lamp that had not been broken in the fall of the chandelier burst from the heat of the rug beneath it. In that sudden bright light Llano Ackers looked directly across the thirty-foot width of the room at Ray Waldron's dim outline.

Both men saw each other at the same instant, both swung their weapons into line at the same split second. The flame lance of Llano's .45 stabbed across to throw its line true with that of Waldron's. Llano felt the slam of a bullet along the right side of his chest, but the wall at his back held his tall frame steady and he thumbed the hammer of his gun until it was empty.

After the third shot Llano saw the flaming arc of Waldron's gun stab obliquely down at the floor. Then Waldron's squat shape was shortening as he doubled at the waist.

Llano heard the cries from the street five minutes later. He heard the crash of the glass at the front door as someone broke through without turning the knob. He had fallen to the floor, face down, and now he raised his empty gun and lined it at the outer parlor doorway, letting it fall at sight of Bob Morley's frail shape appearing there. Then a wave of faintness hit him and he had only a hazy memory of leaning against Bob's shoulder and walking across the room.

They carried him to Doc Moore's office and laid him on the operating bench the medico had a year ago freighted in from Denver. Mary Morley held the chloroform-soaked wad of bandage to his nose and he fought against the sickening sweetness of the drug until she said: "We have to do it, Llano. You have three bullets in you."

He came out of it toward morning, when the lamp in the medico's office had burned low and Mary was beginning to wonder which deep breath would be Llano's last. The first thing he saw, as he opened his eyes, was a hazy picture of the girl's face. Her image cleared, and, as he caught the tenderness of her expression, he felt unsteadiness in his chest.

"It's all over now, Llano," the girl said. "I . . . I'm so proud of you."

He looked up at her and the unmasked quality in his glance made her face take on a rush of color. She said: "I'll get the doctor. He told me to wake him if there was any change."

She had half raised from her chair alongside the bed when his voice spoke its firm, soft drawl. "I don't need a sawbones now."

She understood the meaning behind his words, and, instead of taking the chair again, she sat on the edge of the bed and leaned down and came into his arms.

About the Author

Peter Dawson is the *nom de plume* used by Jonathan Hurff Glidden. He was born in Kewanee, Illinois, and was graduated from the University of Illinois with a degree in English literature. In his career as a Western writer he published sixteen Western novels and wrote over one hundred and twenty Western short novels and short stories for the magazine market. From the beginning he was a dedicated craftsman who revised and polished his fiction until it shone as a fine gem. His Peter Dawson novels are noted for their adept plotting, interesting and well-developed characters, their authentically researched historical backgrounds, and his stylistic flair. During the Second World War, Glidden served with the U.S. Strategic and Tactical Air Force in the United Kingdom. Later in 1950 he served for a time as Assistant to Chief of Station in Germany. After the war, his novels were frequently serialized in *The Saturday Evening Post*. Peter Dawson titles such as *Gunsmoke Graze*, *Royal Gorge*, and *Ruler of the Range* are generally conceded to be among his best titles, although he was an extremely consistent writer, and virtually all his fiction has retained its classic stature among readers of all generations. One of Jon Glidden's finest techniques was his ability, after the fashion of Dickens and Tolstoy, to tell his stories via a series of dramatic vignettes that focus on a wide assortment of different characters, all tending to develop their own lives, situations, and predicaments, while at the same time propelling the general plot of the story toward a suspenseful conclusion. He was no less gifted as a master of the short novel and short story. *Dark Riders of Doom* was the first collection of his Western short novels and stories to be published.

BLOOD TRAIL TO KANSAS

ROBERT J. RANDISI

Ted Shea thinks he is a goner for sure. All the years he's worked to build his Montana spread and fine herd of prime beef means nothing if he can't sell them. And with a vicious rustler and his gang of cutthroats scaring all the hands, no one is willing to take to the trail. Until Dan Parmalee drifts into town. A gunman and gambler with a taste for long odds, he isn't about to let a little hot lead part him from some cold cash. But it doesn't take Dan long to realize this isn't just any run. This is a...*Blood Trail to Kansas*.

ISBN 10: 0-8439-5799-9
ISBN 13: 978-0-8439-5799-0 $5.99 US/$7.99 CAN